UPSIDE ★ DOWN MAGIC

DRAGON OVERNIGHT

by

Sarah
MLYNOWSKI,

Lauren
MYRACLE,

and

Emily
JENKINS

SCHOLASTIC INC.

For everyone who has ever wanted to be a dritten.

Or a skunkephant.

ISBN 978-1-338-27769-2

10 9 8 7 6   22 23

Printed in the U.S.A.   40
First printing 2018

Book design by Abby Dening

Zamboozle! No school for three days!"

Nory Horace bounced and flung her arms over her head. It was a crisp November morning. She had her favorite purple rain boots on, even though it wasn't raining. Her poufy hair was squashed beneath a knitted cap.

The Dunwiddle Magic School parking lot was full of families dropping off their kids. Duffel bags and backpacks were piled by the cheerful blue field-trip bus.

Aunt Margo hugged Nory good-bye. Nory's aunt

was sturdy, pale-skinned, and practical, whereas Nory was wiry, dark-skinned, and lively. "It's a *school* trip," Aunt Margo said. "That's still school."

"Not to me." Nory wiggled out of the hug and started bouncing again. "No math! No poetry analysis! No interpretive dance! And we're going to see *dragons*!"

"Not just see them, *take care of them*," added Marigold Ramos. Marigold was one of Nory's school friends, but not a best friend. She had long dark hair, a leather jacket, woolly yellow gloves, and a warm smile.

"Do you think we'll get to feed them?" Nory asked. "Or pet them? Or ride them? Or cut their toenails? I'd wouldn't mind cutting some dragon toenails. Really, I wouldn't."

"The dragons don't need manicures. They need rehabilitation," said Aunt Margo. "They're in Dragon Haven because they're injured and can't survive in the wild."

"I know," said Nory. "But some will get better and return to their natural habitat, right?"

Aunt Margo nodded. "Yes. And others will live in the wildlife center for good."

"Do you think we can walk them on leashes?" asked Marigold. "Just the little ones, I mean. Not the big ones."

Aunt Margo shook her head, laughing. "I should go. I have a client." She hugged Nory once more. "I'm going to miss you."

Nory grinned. "I'll be too busy petting dragons to be homesick."

"Just don't bring any of them home with you. They're cute when they're little, but they take up *a lot* of room when they're older!" With one last smile, Aunt Margo wrapped her scarf around her neck, tilted herself into flying position, and took off to pick up the latest passenger for her flying taxi service.

Flying was one of the five types of typical magic. Then there were Flares, Fluxers, Fuzzies, and Flickers.

Flyers flew.

Flares worked with fire and heat.

Fluxers could turn themselves into animals.

Fuzzies could talk to and connect with animals.

Flickers could turn invisible or make other things invisible.

But not everybody *had* typical magic that could be neatly described by a word starting with *F*. Nory didn't, and neither did Marigold. Marigold shrank things and couldn't make them big again. Nory was an Upside-Down Fluxer.

When Nory had turned ten, her magic had bubbled up, like everyone's did. But her magic had turned out to be . . . unusual. She didn't flux into everyday animals like kittens, dogs, and goats. Instead, she turned into mixed-up animals. A puppy with squid legs, for example. A squippy! Or a kitten mixed with a dragon—a dritten!

Nory's father, Dr. Stone Horace, was the headmaster of a fancy private magic school called Sage Academy. It was one of the best schools in the country. Nory's older brother and sister went there.

But Nory had flunked the Sage Academy admissions test.

Father had been very, very disappointed in her. That was why he had sent her to live with Aunt Margo. Aunt Margo lived near Dunwiddle Magic School, a public school where an experimental Upside-Down Magic class had just started up. Nory was enrolled there.

Nory's teacher, Ms. Starr, turned out to be awesome. And there were only seven other fifth-grade kids in the Upside-Down Magic class, so everybody got a lot of individual attention.

In the parking lot, Elliott Cohen and Pepper Phan came over to Nory and Marigold. Elliott was Nory's best friend. He was an Upside-Down Flare. He froze things instead of heating them.

Pepper was Nory's other best friend. Pepper was tiny, especially in her enormous puffy coat. She had come to see them off, since she wasn't going on the trip. The Dragon Haven people thought her magic posed too much of a risk. Pepper was a Fierce, which was a rare kind of Upside-Down Fuzzy. If a typical Fuzzy met a scurry of squirrels, her animal magic would get them eating peanuts out of her hand in no time. But instead of charming animals, Pepper frightened them. Squirrels squinted their tiny eyes and ran away. Hedgehogs dove into holes. Chickadees pooped in terror.

"I still can't believe you're not coming," Nory said.

"I just can't," Pepper said. "If I fierced an injured dragon, it could hurt itself more. If I fierced a flying dragon, it could escape."

Nory pouted. "I know. But it's so unfair!"

Pepper shrugged. "Anyway, I get the days off from school. Have double fun for me, all right?" Pepper gave Nory such a quick hug that Nory didn't have time to hug her back. Then she was gone.

Nory, Marigold, and Elliott were silent and solemn for a moment. Then Nory forced herself to look on the bright side. "Do you think we'll get to stay up super late?" she asked her friends.

"The boys' cabin is planning ghost stories one night," said Elliott, nodding.

"We'll get to see Ms. Starr in her pajamas!"

Nory said to Marigold. "What kind do you think she wears?"

"Hot pink," said Elliott.

"Candy-apple red," said Marigold.

Ms. Starr always wore bright colors. Here she came now, in blue jeans, bright green sneakers, and an electric-orange jacket that looked great against her dark skin. Above her floated Andres Padillo on a leash.

Andres was an Upside-Down Flyer. Like typical Flyers, he could fly, but he went a lot higher than other Flyers his age. The upside-down part was that he couldn't *stop* flying.

At all.

Half the time, Andres wore a backpack full of bricks to make sure he didn't float off into the sky. Right now, his brickpack was being carried by Nurse Riley, the school nurse, who was coming on the field trip as a second chaperone. Today was the first time Nory had seen him out of his scrubs. He wore cargo pants and a brown woolly sweater. He looked tough,

Nory thought. Like a mountain man instead of a tenderhearted goof who doled out cough drops and Band-Aids.

Nurse Riley nodded at Ms. Starr and heaved Andres's brickpack over his shoulder. He made it halfway to the luggage compartment of the bus before dropping the pack and bracing his hands against his legs. "Wow, that's heavy," he muttered.

"We should help Nurse Riley load the bags," Nory declared.

She, Marigold, and Elliott formed an assembly line, passing bags from one person to the next until they reached Nurse Riley. He arranged everything in the storage compartment under the bus.

Sebastian joined them. As usual, he was dressed a little formally, as if he were going to a tea party instead of a wildlife refuge. He had pale skin and bright red cheeks, and he wore a cone around his head, the kind dogs wore after having surgery.

Sebastian was an Upside-Down Flicker. Typical Flickers could make themselves or other things invisible. Sebastian, on the other hand, could see invisible things, like sound waves. Music was beautiful, he told the others, with intricate patterns. But big crowds and upset tempers hurt his eyes and gave him headaches.

That's why he wore his cone when it was going to be a noisy trip. It blocked out some, though not all, of the sound waves that bothered him.

Finally, it was time to go. They had an entire school bus to themselves. Nory skipped to the last row and Elliott sat down beside her. She leaned back against the vinyl seat. Her stomach felt fizzy with excitement, and she wondered if it was possible for a person to feel her own eyes sparkling.

She turned to her left. "Hey, Elliott—are my eyes sparkling?"

"Huh?"

"Never mind," Nory said. She was sure they were.

2

Hey!" Andres called as his leash pulled against his wrist. He had been floating on his back, looking up at the lovely, boring, always-there sky. Now he flipped over—and his pulse rocketed.

The doors of the bus were closed.

Closed!

Ms. Starr, who held the other end of his leash, was *in* the bus.

And the bus was moving.

"HEY!" Andres yelped. The sound ripped out of

him. The bus was picking up speed. Everyone down there had forgotten about him.

He thought about the world that way now. Everyone else was *down there*. Ever since his upside-down magic kicked in during fourth grade, the world had split in two: up here (sky) and down there (ground).

It would have been okay if he'd had company in the sky. But the typical Flyers rarely bothered to talk to him, and none of his upside-down magic friends could fly at all, unless you counted Nory when she had wings.

The bus picked up speed as it crossed the school parking lot.

Really, people? Andres thought. *Really?!*

Luckily, the speed and wind pushed him down until he was level with the windows of the bus. Sitting in the last row he could see Nory, smiling blissfully and doing weird things with her eyes.

He rapped on the glass. "Hey!"

Nory startled at the sound. She turned toward him and beamed. "Andres!" she called, and waved.

She. Actually. Waved.

Andres scowled. "Let me in! You guys *forgot* me!"

Nory's brow furrowed, and then her mouth opened into a perfect O. She dashed up the aisle.

The brakes squealed. The bus came to such a hard stop that Andres was flung forward.

"Ow," he cried, rubbing his wrist where the leash had dug in. It was probably sprained. It was probably broken! It would probably drop off his arm like a dead fish, and Nory and the others wouldn't even notice!

Would his dismembered dead-fish hand float up, like the rest of him? Or would it fall to earth? Either way was bad, and Andres felt very unlucky.

Ms. Starr pushed through the doors of the bus and ran to him, the handle-end of his leash around her own wrist. "I'm so sorry, Andres. I got distracted by Sebastian. And, oh, I guess I'm a little nervous. It's my first field trip and my first year teaching, you know. A million things are running through my brain. Anway, I'm truly sorry. I can't apologize enough." She tugged him onto the bus.

Andres rolled his eyes. "It's fine. I'm used to it."

Ms. Starr released the leash now that they were inside. "Well, I'm glad you're okay. Get your brick-pack on and find a seat," she instructed. "Don't forget to buckle up!"

The bus lurched forward.

Andres flew immediately to the top of the bus and bumped his head and back on its roof. He looked for his brickpack. Where was it?

He could ask Ms. Starr, but Sebastian was having a crisis, whimpering and rocking back and forth. The plastic cone circling his head rocked back and forth with him.

"Too zippy," Sebastian moaned. "Too much noise."

Ms. Starr patted his back. Nurse Riley suggested he close his eyes.

"You don't understand!" Sebastian complained. "Closing my eyes helps a little, but the light still leaks in. I can't believe I forgot to pack my blindfold. The vibrations of the bus engine, the grinding gears . . . they *hurt*!"

Ms. Starr glanced at Nurse Riley for help. "Does anyone have a scarf we can use for a blindfold? The cone isn't enough!"

The bus took a right out of the parking lot, and Andres made his way to the back of the vehicle. He really needed his brickpack. It would weigh him down and keep him in a seat. He looked. And looked.

Oh, no.

It wasn't here.

The bus made a turn and Andres bounced painfully across the ceiling. "Can someone help?" he called.

Willa Ingeborg jumped from her seat and leapt for the leash. "Got you!"

The bus bumped over a pothole. The leash ripped from Willa's hand, and Andres flew back to the roof.

"Lost you," Willa said miserably. Tears welled in her eyes. Then large, round raindrops drip-drip-dropped over Willa and her seatmate, Marigold. Willa was an Upside-Down Flare. Instead of fire magic, she had water magic. She could make it rain, but only indoors. And when she got upset, she often rained by accident.

Marigold quickly covered her hearing aid so it wouldn't get wet.

"Ms. Starr, did you bring any umbrellas?" Nory asked. "Ms. Starr?"

But Ms. Starr was all the way in the front with Sebastian and couldn't hear over the noise.

"Hold on," Elliott said. "I can help." With a flourish, he fisted his hand and then flung out his fingers. Willa's rain turned to hail.

Marigold stood up. "I'm changing seats." She walked over to an empty bench where the hail wasn't falling.

Nory took her hat off and handed it to Marigold, just in case.

Up on the ceiling, Andres was scared. The bus was rattling down the road, and the roof was digging into his spine. "Still here!" he called. "Still need help!"

Bax Kapoor looked up at him. Bax was an Upside-Down Fluxer. He had very short hair, medium-brown skin, and a tendency to wear T-shirts that suggested rock bands, sharks, or pirates. Instead of fluxing into animals, he fluxed into *things*. Rocks, mainly. Once a piano. Occasionally a swivel chair.

"Hey," he said now. "I have an idea!"

"I KNOW!" Nory cried, bolting up. "I'll flux into a koat!"

"A kitten plus a goat? How would *that* help?" asked Bax.

"Because goats eat hail!"

"The hail is on the bottom of the bus," Bax pointed out. "Andres is stuck on the top."

"Also, no, they don't," said Elliott.

"Sure they do. Goats eat everything!" said Nory.

"Also, why add kitten into it?" Elliott said.

"For size, silly!" said Nory. "Do you really think a *goat* on a bus would be a good idea? Hmm?"

Andres saw Nory do that thing where she scrunched her face and kind of . . . wavered. She did that when she started fluxing.

"Nory, koat is not a good plan!" Bax said, but Nory's eyes bulged, her muscles rippled, and her hair did that creepy thing where it disappeared into her scalp. Soon she had the body and tail of a black kitten and the legs and head of small goat. Her tremendous goat horns almost toppled her over.

"Baaa," Koat-Nory said. "Baaa-aaa!" She chomped quickly through her seat belt and wobbled toward the marble-like balls of hail that were rolling about on the floor of the bus. Bax clapped his hand to his forehead.

"Guys?" Andres called. The bus was turning a corner and he was banging against the roof. "Still need help!"

Koat-Nory slipped. Her legs splayed in four different directions, and she squealed.

"For the love of vegetables," Andres heard Bax mutter. Bax unbuckled, rose from his seat, and grabbed Andres's leash. Unlike Willa, he didn't let go. He hauled Andres down and pushed him into a seat.

"I'm gonna flux now," Bax said. "Sorry if this is a little weird."

Suddenly, Bax was a rock. A very large rock. And he was on Andres's lap.

Relief! Andres was pinned to his seat. He could feel the tug of his magic wanting to lift him up, but he couldn't float away. Rock-Bax was holding him down.

Up at the front of the bus, Ms. Starr had managed to settle down Sebastian at last. She'd taken off his head cone and wrapped Nurse Riley's woolly sweater around his head. Now Sebastian rocked gently back and forth in his seat, his legs drawn up and his arms around his shins.

Ms. Starr turned now to the chaos behind her, "Nory! Willa! What's happening back there?"

With a pop, Nory fluxed back into her girl self. She clambered to stand on her two human feet, holding on to the back of a bench. "Nothing, Ms. Starr. All's good!"

"Please sit down, Nory," said Ms. Starr. "And fasten your seat belt!"

Nory had chewed through her seat belt, but she found a new place and obeyed.

"Willa, you seem to be raining," said Ms. Starr.

"A little," Willa said in a small voice.

"And Elliott, are you freezing the rain into hail?"

"Kind of?"

Ms. Starr wiped her brow. "Well, I suppose that makes sense. Go ahead and keep up the freezing until Willa gets calm."

Elliott nodded.

Ms. Starr encouraged Willa to breathe deeply and to recite a poem they had all memorized. It was about mermaids. By the third verse of the poem, the magic rain cloud vanished.

Ms. Starr counted their heads. Her brow wrinkled. "Students, where's Bax?"

Andres pointed to his lap.

"Ah." Ms. Starr nodded to herself. "Okay, then."

Life with a bunch of wonkos is tough, Andres thought. *There's so much to worry about.*

Nory tapped him on the arm. She leaned across the aisle and held out a box of choco fire trucks.

He took two.

"Sorry about all that," she said. "Are you okay?"

"Yeah, sure."

Nory passed out choco fire trucks to the others. "I'll save a couple for Bax," she whispered, patting Rock-Bax in Andres's lap.

Andres looked out the window and ate his fire-truck chocolates slowly, making them last.

3

They ate packed lunches. Nory had leftover pizza and two tangerines. The bus wound its way through Angel Canyon. The rugged two-lane mountain highway was the last leg of their journey. Majestic cliffs rose on either side of them. Wow, it was beautiful. Nory felt small.

The mountain highway topped out at last. Grand script was chiseled into an impressive stone arch. It read: DRAGON HAVEN. It was the entrance of the dragon rescue, protection, and preservation center.

The forest stretched out in front of them, the fall leaves shining in the sunlight.

"We're here!" cried Ms. Starr. Everyone piled out of the bus except for Andres and Rock-Bax, who stayed in their seats while Nurse Riley tended to them.

Outside, excited chatter flew back and forth. Sebastian unwrapped Nurse Riley's sweater from over his eyes and put back on his head cone. Elliott helped him adjust it. The bus driver unloaded backpacks, duffels, and sleeping bags, piling them in front of the Welcome Center.

"Hello, campers!" someone called out.

Nory turned and saw a regal woman flying toward them. She stopped and hovered a couple of feet in the air. She was thin and had a long neck. Shiny black hair hung like a bolt of silk down her back. She wore blue scrubs, like a doctor. "My name is Dr. Miriam Cho," the woman continued, "but you may call me Mo. I am the chief dragonologist at Dragon Haven. I'm honored to welcome you to our center."

"Hi!" blurted Nory. "I'm Nory!" Andres shot her

a look, but Nory didn't care. There was a real drag-onologist, right in front of her! Wearing actual ugly blue pants!

Nory had thought all dragonologists worked in dense, uninhabited forests, wild wetlands, and vast sandy plains, riding around in safari cars with teams of photographers. She'd thought all of them were Fuzzies, too. That's what it seemed like in the educational film on dragons that Ms. Starr had made them watch. But here was Mo, a real live Flyer dragonologist with glamorous hair!

"You Dunwiddle students are one of two school groups we have with us right now," Mo continued, "and there will be plenty of time for introductions later. We'll wait for the other group to arrive."

The other group? Nory thought. *What other group?*

Nory's eyes flew to Elliott, then to Ms. Starr. Both looked as confused as Nory.

One of the reasons Nory had been so excited about this overnight trip was that it was going to be just Ms. Starr's Upside-Down Magic class. No other kids from Dunwiddle would be there. No mean Flares, no cliquey Fuzzies, no intimidating older kids. Nory didn't want another group of students at Dragon Haven. The idea made her nervous.

"Come along," said Mo. "I'll give you a brief tour of our facility." She gestured behind her. "That, of course, is the Welcome Center. Pamphlets, photo opportunities, a gift store with books and postcards." She sniffed. "It's the sort of nonsense our rescue center has to have in order to remain funded. The more interesting artifacts are in the Great Hall, where we have exhibits and a reference library."

She headed across a grassy field. Nory and the others followed. The air was chilly. The silence of the dragon reserve felt very different to the bustle of town life.

Nory peeked at Sebastian. The sounds of the forest were so quiet and pretty that he had taken off his head cone.

Then a shriek pierced the air. It was high and wild and terrifying, but also glorious.

"That's a Bramble Dragon," Mo said. "What a noise, eh? She was caught by hunters and sold to people who thought they wanted a baby dragon for a pet. Can you imagine? Wild animals should never be pets. Foolish, foolish people. They called us after she burned their house down." Mo sighed. "She's rehabilitating nicely, though."

The dragonologist picked up her pace and pointed to the right. "Several miles to the east is a facility for the study and rehabilitation of river dragons. All the dragons here are sick, injured, or orphaned. They're unable to live in the wild. Our goal is to help them get better and then release them to natural habitats. And while they're here, students and scientists can study them."

Mo then showed them the most important areas of the preserve: a veterinary clinic, a fireproof room for injured fire-breathing dragons, and a building she said was a hatchery. When a clutch of eggs was found abandoned, she explained, dragon whelps could be hatched in an incubator.

Next came wooded areas with clearly marked paths that were safe for students to explore, a Great Hall full of exhibits, and the cafeteria.

"Now I'll show you your lodgings," said Mo. "The girls will share one cabin, along with Ms. Starr. The boys will bunk with—?"

"Me," Nurse Riley said, lifting a meaty hand. "Felix."

Felix! Nory grinned. She hadn't known Nurse Riley even *had* a first name. She'd kind of thought his first name was *Nurse*.

In the girls' cabin were three bunk beds. Nory claimed the bunk closest to the window. She scrambled to the top and wished suddenly for Pepper. Marigold and Willa would, of course, be together. Ms. Starr was taking the third bunk for herself. Pepper would have been Nory's friend for the bottom bunk, but she wasn't here.

"Check it out!" Willa cried, looking through a screened window.

"Nory, come!" Marigold said, joining Willa. "It's the other student group. They're here."

Ugh. Nory hid her face in the pillow of her top bunk and tried not to think about these strangers who were arriving. They might be mean about upside-down magic. She didn't want them to ruin her wonderful dragon overnight.

"They look the same age as us," reported Marigold.

"They're wearing uniforms," said Willa.

"Skirts for the girls," said Marigold.

"And ties for the boys."

"There are, like, nearly fifty kids! The girls are going into five cabins. And one of them is a—wow, she's a really good Fluxer. She just turned into an elephant."

"No fifth grader can do elephant," said Nory into her pillow. "She must be an eighth grader."

"She has a patch on her duffel bag that says 'Fifth-Grade Squad Goals,'" said Marigold.

"Well, she's a show-off, then," said Nory.

"You can do elephant," said Willa encouragingly.

"No," said Nory. "I can add a bit of elephant to other animals. Skunkephant. Bluebird-elephant. Neither's the same as a proper elephant, though. Proper elephant needs sustained trunk and jumbo size. It's harder than it seems."

"*I* think fluxing into a skunkephant is harder than it seems," Marigold said loyally. "Anyway, since when have you been afraid of hard things?"

Marigold had a good point. Nory pushed herself up from her pillow and sat back on her heels. "Since never."

And to prove it, she jumped from the top bunk to the floor, landing on both feet.

4

Nurse Riley had left Andres's brickpack in the parking lot back at Dunwiddle.

Really.

The nurse had been over-the-top apologetic. And he'd offered Andres his own backpack to use. But there were no bricks to put in it. Elliott, Sebastian, and Bax (who'd turned back into a boy, with Nurse Riley's help) had gone out searching for small but heavy stones.

They hadn't found anything that would work.

Now Andres floated above the UDM boys as they

trekked to the Great Hall for orientation. Nurse Riley held the leash. He had promised to, as a way of making it up to Andres. But Andres felt like he was back in preschool, the rowdy kid forced to hold the teacher's hand on walks while the rest of the kids skipped ahead on their own.

When they reached the Great Hall, the girls were already there. The space felt like a brand-new barn that had been decorated like a library. The room had extremely high ceilings and wood walls. At the center of the ceiling was a dome painted with an ornate mural of a Barnacle Dragon. There were huge, overlapping carpets, and shelves and shelves of books. Andres spotted Nory flipping through an illustrated tome that lived on a special bookstand.

"Sea dragons!" Nory exclaimed, bouncing on her toes. "Look, Willa! There are so many kinds of sea dragons! I only knew about Seaweed Dragons and Barnacle Dragons. You know, the ones that are always in storybooks. But there are like fifteen different species! Havoline-Dex, Freddo, Reef, Icebreath . . ."

"I know about Icebreath!" said Andres. "I did a report on them in fourth grade, actually."

No one heard him.

"They only live near volcanoes," he continued. "The ice breathing is actually an adaptation that kept them alive during a period of big volcanic eruptions."

Still, no one heard him. Nory, Willa, and Elliott weren't even talking about sea dragons anymore. Now they were looking at the dragons of the wilderness.

Mo, the dragonologist, flew to the top of the room, hovering above the group. She arced easily past the sturdy wooden beams that crisscrossed the high ceiling. She counted the students, waved at Andres on his leash, and lowered herself to the floor. Then she sat down on the carpet, crossing her legs. She called for the others to gather around her. They did. Andres floated above.

"I'm glad to have you here," Mo began. "The rest of the staff asked me to welcome you on their behalf.

They can't be here because caring for our dragons takes a lot of work. Dragons are not pets. They're wild animals, and you must all remember that, at all times."

"Has anyone ever been eaten?" Elliott blurted.

Mo regarded him coolly. "Most dragons are omnivorous. They eat meat, but they don't seek out humans for food any more than bears do. To be safe, we make sure that other food is always available."

She shifted her gaze to include the others. "Some of you will be given the chance to help with the feeding of the dragons. Other activities include river dragon research, dragon hatchery, and care of whelps—"

"What's a whelp?" Willa asked.

"A whelp is a baby dragon. Most breeds are very small at first. They don't have a big growth spurt until six months or so, which means that even the ferocious ones are pretty cute," said Mo, smiling. "We also offer rehabilitation work with flying dragons, a tour of the hatchery, and a chance to feed the Bubble Dragons who live in our lake."

Andres looked at his friends. Sebastian's face was bright and interested. Elliott was chewing on his thumbnail like he was nervous. Bax's face was blank, as usual, but he was drumming his fingertips rapidly on his forearms. Maybe he was secretly excited.

"Dragon Haven is a unique place," Mo said in a wrapping-up tone. "You'll see dragons in a way you'd never see them in a zoo—up close and in as natural a habitat as we can provide." She rose to her feet, a pretzel unfolding with grace and balance.

"Dinner will be in one hour," she announced. She swept her arm to indicate the exhibits and displays that filled the Great Hall. "Until then, enjoy." She left the room.

Andres watched as the UDM kids milled around the hall again.

Nurse Riley looked up. "Is there something you'd like to see? I can take you."

"No. That's okay." Andres felt awkward.

"I'd love to check out the display of dragon

skeletons," said Nurse Riley. "Would it be all right if I tied your leash to this chair?"

"Go ahead."

"Just for a minute or two," said Nurse Riley. "I'll be right back."

"Take your time."

Nurse Riley jogged off and tapped Bax on the shoulder. The two of them went over to look at skeletons of tiny dragons of different breeds, lined up in a glass case.

Andres was alone in the air.

Again.

5

There was an hour till dinner and Nory couldn't wait to move. She tapped Elliott on the shoulder. "Want to explore?"

"Of course!"

They told Ms. Starr they'd be at the cafeteria for dinner and stepped outside into a bright, autumn-scented afternoon. In Dragon Haven, there were no paved roads. The fallen leaves crunched beneath their feet.

"I wonder when we'll see dragons," said Elliott. "I'm kind of scared, to tell you the truth."

"Why?"

"Teeth, fangs, claws. Teeth, fire breath, enormous jaws. Oh, and also teeth," said Elliott. "Isn't it obvious?"

"I'm not scared," said Nory. "I'm kind of thrilled."

They started on a trail through the woods. The trees stretched taller and the shadows loomed darker.

Thud!

Hisssss.

"Um, what was that?" Elliott asked.

"I don't know," said Nory.

"Do you think it was a dragon?"

"No."

"But this is Dragon Haven!"

"Yeah, but they won't be loose in the forest, Elliott. Mo said the paths were safe for students to walk on."

"Then do you think it's a fox?"

"Foxes don't hiss."

"A snake?"

"Maybe."

"Should I be ready to freeze it?"

Nory nodded. "Be ready to freeze it."

Hisss! The sound came again.

Hisssssssss!

And then . . .

Meow! Mrwowow? Meow!

Nory and Elliott stepped into a clearing. There were seven kittens, hissing and meowing at each other. Plus two yarnballs, and a nice little kittenball court, with wooden railings around a green field and a tower with a basket in the center. They had stumbled onto a kittenball game.

Kittenball was a sport Nory played at Dunwiddle. It was for Fluxers, and when they played it, they fluxed into kittens. The goal was to work together to pass and climb your yarnball up the tower and drop it in the basket. But meanwhile, the opposing team tries to stop you from scoring by unspooling your yarn.

Nory loved kittenball, but she knew the kittens here had to be the strangers from the other school.

As she and Elliot approached, the kittens stopped meowing and tail-whacking. They turned up their cute little faces to look at the new arrivals.

"Cool!" said Elliott, squatting down on his heels to talk to them. "Are you playing kittenball?" He laughed awkwardly. "Um, duh. Of course you're playing kittenball. I love kittenball! I'm Elliott, and this is Nory. I'm a—well, I'm *not* a Fluxer. Heh heh. But Nory is. Can she play with you? It looks like you need an extra kitten. What's the score? Who's on the blue team? Did I say I'm Elliott? Have you seen any dragons yet? Do you know if there are any dragons in the woods? Like, running loose? Oh, sorry. I guess I'm interrupting your scrimmage. Sorry."

The kittens didn't answer . . . *because they were kittens.* They couldn't talk until they switched back to human form.

Nory felt embarrassed that Elliott was babbling, but she *did* kind of want to play. She had been working with a fluxing tutor and taking kittenball classes since the start of the school year. She was able to hold the shape of an ordinary black kitten for fifteen or twenty minutes before things started to get unusual. And her tail-whacking was getting pretty strong.

One of the kittens—a calico—popped back into human form. She straightened up, pushed her sweaty bangs off her forehead, and grinned.

"I'm Mitali," she said. She had bright eyes, a big smile, light brown skin, and dark brown hair cut in a swingy bob. She was wearing green sweats and a big white T-shirt. Nory could tell from her ragged cuticles that she bit her fingernails.

"Hi," Nory said. "I'm Nory. Which you already know, because Elliott told you."

"Wanna join?" Mitali asked. "We really could use an eighth."

Nory liked the girl immediately, but she still felt awkward. Was Mitali the Fluxer who could do elephant? It seemed likely. Calico was the hardest of all kitten colors to master, so she was obviously a strong Fluxer.

"I can referee," Elliott volunteered.

Mitali swept her hand toward her friends. There were three black kittens, a butterscotch, a fluffy white, and a gray tabby. "That's Fuchsia, Suki, Theresa-May, Anemone, Yarrow, and Fred. Black cats with the white yarnball and patterned cats with the blue. You in for the black cat team?"

Nory hesitated. She was pretty sure she could hold her kitten shape, but she felt strange with these new kids. Should she say right away that her magic was upside down? And Elliott's? Or was there no need to talk about it unless it came up?

"Come on, we won't bite," Mitali said. "Except for Fuchsia." She shot Fuchsia a teasing look. "The black kittens really do need a fourth."

With a shiver and jolt, Nory fluxed before she could change her mind. Mitali fluxed back into a calico, and the game was on! Kitten-Nory pounced and caught the blue yarn between her paws. The white fluffy one—Kitten-Fuchsia—bounded after her and tried to wrestle the ball away.

Kitten-Mitali snagged the loose end of the white yarn and pulled, unraveling almost the whole thing. *No!* Kitten-Nory bit down on the snippet of white yarn. Kitten-Mitali yanked it free, and was about to tail-whack it so it unrolled toward Kitten-Fuchsia, but Kitten-Nory pounced onto what was left of the white yarn ball and rolled over and over, wrapping the yarn around her furry belly. It was a move called a Yaggle, and Nory's coach had taught it to her just the previous week.

Kitten-Mitali was not happy about the Yaggle. She mewed in frustration, and a short burst of fire came out of her kitten mouth.

What?!

A kitten who breathed fire?

Pop!

Girl-Nory found herself sitting on her bottom in the field. She was so astonished, she'd fluxed back into human form.

She had *never* seen a kitten breathe fire. She herself breathed fire when she mixed up kitten and dragon to become a dritten, but then she had wings and fangs and claws. The fire and the fangs and the wings came from the dragon. What Mitali had done was just a regular kitten with fire breath.

Did that mean Mitali's magic was upside down?

Mitali fluxed back. So did Fuchsia, who revealed herself to be tall and redheaded, with super-pale skin and a hawklike face. "Mitali!" she scolded. "No flaring. We all agreed."

"It's not against the kittenball rules!" Mitali argued.

"That's because kittenball is for *Fluxers*," snapped Fuchsia. "They didn't think to put it in the rules. You practically singed my fur off. There's not even a fire extinguisher out here." She rolled her eyes and stalked off.

Three of the other kittens immediately jumped the railing that surrounded the kittenball court and followed Fuchsia down the path. The other two kittens looked hesitant, as if they weren't sure what to do. Then they sat down and washed their paws with their tongues, pretending not to notice any awkwardness.

"You can tell us," said Nory. "Are you upside down?"

"I'm sorry," Mitali said, blushing. "Fuchsia's right. I'm very competitive and I flare when the going gets tough." She looked straight at Nory. "You're a good kittenballer."

"Thanks," said Nory. "But how did you do that fire?"

Mitali smiled. "I'm not upside down. I'm a double talent. Flare plus Fluxer."

"Oh," Nory said, feeling her heart drop. "That's cool."

"You do a really cute kitten," Mitali said generously. "I liked how you did your whiskers."

"You should show her," said Elliott.

"Show me what?" asked Mitali.

"Nory should show you *her* fire-breathing."

"Are you a double talent, too?" Mitali looked excited.

"I have upside-down magic," Nory said quickly. "We all do—all of us who are here from my school. I'm an Upside-Down Fluxer."

"Oh." Mitali looked over at the two kittens, who were now chasing their tails and pretending not to listen. "I never met anyone with upside-down magic before. Is it hard?"

"Sometimes," said Nory.

"Sometimes it's just super awkward," said Elliott. "And it's harder for some people than for others. Depending on their magic and how it works, and their family's attitudes, and whether other kids give them a hard time . . ." He trailed off.

"Other times it's awesome," said Nory. "Or surprising. Or . . . magical, I guess."

Mitali nodded. Nory realized this was exactly what she'd been worried about—kids looking at her and asking about her upside-down magic. But Mitali's face was so sweet that Nory relaxed.

"Can I see?" said Mitali. "The upside-down flux-ing? And the fire-breathing?"

"Show her," said Elliott.

So Nory fluxed. First back into a kitten, and then *pop-pop-pop!* Her wings sprouted, her teeth felt large in her mouth, and her claws became scaly and long. She flapped her wings and swooped around, zipping across the clearing. She dive-bombed the two remaining kittens, who were staring up at her. Then she perched on a low branch and breathed out a puff of fire.

"Whoa!" Mitali's eyes were huge.

Nory leapt off the branch, landing easily, the way kittens do. Then she popped back into her girl shape. "Yeah," she said proudly. "Not a double talent, but I do breathe fire!"

"I'll say!" Mitali exclaimed. "What *was* that thing?"

"A dritten. Half dragon, half kitten."

"Nory. Seriously. That is the most awesome fluxing I have ever seen in my entire life." Mitali turned to the two kittens. "That was awesome, right?" The two kittens looked very, very nervous, but they nodded.

Nory glowed. She enjoyed her upside-down magic much more now than she used to. She could manage it better, and some animal forms were quite fun. She also knew she wielded a big amount of power. But the different magic could still be really embarrassing. Koat-Nory had eaten Aunt Margo's bedspread just last week.

"You can still play two against two," said Elliott, reaching down into the kittenball court to pick up the blue yarnball and roll it back together. "There's half an hour left before dinner."

Mitali turned to the remaining kittens. "Anemone? Fred? You in?"

The kittens ran to the center of the court. Mitali fluxed. Nory fluxed. Elliott refereed. The game was back on.

6

The leash came loose. Nurse Riley hadn't secured it well, and the pull of Andres's involuntary flying had set it free. Andres found himself floating up, up, up—until he rested against the painted dragon on the room's high dome.

He looked down to realize nearly everyone was leaving. They were trotting merrily off, exiting the Great Hall in a noisy flurry of hunger and excitement. Even Nurse Riley and Bax.

Andres called for Marigold and Willa, the last

two in the room, but they were deep in conversation as they walked out of the Great Hall.

"Well, hello," Andres said to the dragon painted on the ceiling.

The dragon was silent.

"Guess it's just you and me, then, huh?"

The dragon remained silent.

"Just me?"

Andres had his back pressed to the ceiling, just like he naturally did when he was off his leash. At home, when he wanted to move around, he often pressed the soles of his feet to the ceiling so he could jump down and grab a piece of furniture. All the furniture in his house had been bolted to the floor so that he could use it this way. Holding on to the bolted furniture, his feet would fly up, but he could reach an apple from a bowl, get a book he needed for his homework, things like that.

Andres tried it now, jumping off the ceiling of the Great Hall. He hoped to grasp the top shelf of a large and heavy bookcase. But the ceiling was so high, he couldn't get anywhere near it. The only thing he could reach—just barely—were the exposed beams that extended along the length of the Great Hall's ceiling.

He had to jump four times, but finally he was able to grab one of the beams with his hands. It was round and thick, and his body whipped around it, as if he were a trapeze artist. The world flew by so fast that it was a blur. Andres let go, rocketing faceup to the opposite side of the room. This time the front of his body came to rest against the ceiling the way his back usually did.

He flipped himself over and jumped again. This time he was ready. He swung around the beam on purpose, letting go just in time to send his body hurtling toward the eastern wall of the room feet first. He bent his knees to cushion his impact as he hit the wall. Then, with a powerful shove, back he zoomed. He flung his hands above his head and grabbed the beam once more. He swung around one-handed this time, extending his legs in a straight line. Bouncing off the wall, he held himself on the beam with his feet floating over his head.

It felt great, this kind of magical gymnastics. He swung so he could push off the wall again and jumped with his knees and chest together, forming a tight ball. He bounced off the wall with his bottom, as he'd planned. The impact made him laugh.

"Ha!" he heard, and panicked. Someone else had laughed as well. Someone standing on the floor below.

Then came more laughter. From *several* some-ones.

Andres floated to the ceiling and looked down. There were four kids he had never seen before: two boys and two girls. The kids from the other school had arrived. They were wearing white shirts and blue school-uniform jackets.

Drat.

"Don't stop now!" the taller of the girls said.

Andres cringed. He hated the way the students with typical magic at Dunwiddle School made fun of him. Some of them, anyway. Would these kids be the same?

"Did we, like, mess up your flow?" the tall girl asked. A quick glance told Andres that she wasn't joking. Her brow was furrowed, and she was chewing on her lower lip. "What you were doing—so cool," she said. The others nodded. "Are you . . . ? Oh, gosh, this is going to sound rude."

"What?" Andres asked suspiciously.

"How old are you? Are you, like, a high schooler who's just, um, short? Not that there's anything wrong with that! We can't help what size we are!" The girl flung out her arms. "Look at me. I'm extremely tall!"

"I'm ten," Andres said.

"I'm ten, too!" said the girl. She wore wire-rim glasses, and rows of tight brown braids framed her face, which was almost exactly the same color as her hair. She did indeed tower over her classmates.

"My name is Phoebe," she said.

"I'm Andres."

"We can only go three feet in the air," said Phoebe, gesturing at the kids around her. "And we're just learning to change directions quickly and to play flyball. How did you learn to do all that? Where do you go to school?"

"Dunwiddle."

"I'm majorly impressed," one of the guys said. He was white and shrimpy, the opposite of tall Phoebe. "In fact I might say my brain exploded just now, watching you."

Andres couldn't believe it. These kids thought he was a good Flyer.

An amazing Flyer.

And maybe he was, in his way. He easily went way higher than three feet. He knew most fifth-grade Flyers couldn't do that. Flyers also got tired easily, and Andres flew with no effort at all. He even flew while sleeping. Now he had found ways to swing and flip, in this wonderful high-ceilinged room. It did seem like some amazing possibilities might be opening up.

But what these new kids didn't know was that Andres couldn't get down.

The small boy waved. "I'm Tip, by the way." He held out his hand, as if to shake.

Andres sighed.

He couldn't hide it. Others could pretend to be typical at least for a little while, but he never could. Plus, Andres had been brought up with manners. He couldn't leave Tip there, with an outstretched hand.

He jumped from the ceiling to catch a beam. Then he scooched himself around on the beam so he could jump off it toward the floor. He leapt and got just low enough to shake Tip's hand.

Oh, no.

Tip didn't weigh nearly enough to hold him down. They rose together, Andres's feet over his head, his magic pulling Tip up, up, up to the ceiling.

"Superlative." Tip grinned, looking down at the floor over his shoulder. "I have never been this high except one time when I took a flying taxi service!"

Andres's mind was racing. He couldn't keep holding Tip's hand forever. But Tip couldn't fly above three feet.

"I'm scared I'll drop you," said Andres. "Your hand is getting sweaty."

"Just cruise back down and release me," said Tip happily. "It's cool. Sorry about the sweat."

"I can't," Andres confessed.

"What?"

"I don't go down. I *can't* go down."

An expression of understanding crossed Phoebe's face below. "*Ohhh.* You have wonky magic."

Andres nodded. "Only we don't say *wonky*. It's more polite to say *different* or *unusual* instead. Or *upside down*."

Phoebe flushed. "I'm sorry. I didn't know."

"Don't drop me," said Tip. He sounded anxious now. "What are we going to do?"

Phoebe floated up three feet. So did the two other Flyers. "I think you should push off the ceiling to one of the beams, and from the beam toward the floor," Phoebe told Andres. "We'll grab Tip. If that works, we'll try to grab you, and maybe all three of us can keep you down."

And that was what they did. Andres pushed off the ceiling, then off the beam. He passed off Tip to Phoebe and her friends. As soon as Andres let go of Tip's hand, gravity worked on Tip just like it did on the others. He wobbled unsteadily for a moment, but Phoebe helped him regain his balance. After that, he floated three feet up, very nicely.

"Can you catch me now?" Andres called down from the beam.

"We can," said the boy who hadn't spoken yet. "I'm Tomás, by the way. But I was hoping we could watch you fly a little more, like with the flips and stuff."

"Me, too," added the other girl. "I'm Lark."

"You really want me to keep going?" said Andres.

"I'm just getting the hang of this, so you know. I don't really know what I'm doing."

"If you don't mind, I think we'd all like to see what you can do," said Phoebe. "Then we can help you get down. How will you get to the cafeteria?"

"We have to use this leash," said Andres. "It should be okay as long as someone heavier than Tip holds it."

"Cool," said Phoebe. "I can do that."

The other four Flyers sat cross-legged, three feet off the floor, leaning back on their hands and looking up at Andres as he practiced. He jumped off walls and swung around the beams of the Great Hall, playing with his reverse gravitational pull.

"Man, you're going to be famous one day!" cried Phoebe. "The whole world is going to know who you are."

"I'm going to tell everyone I knew you when," said Tip. "I'm going to say, 'He shook my sweaty hand. That guy flew me up to the ceiling when I was only ten!'"

Andres wasn't sure. But for the first time since his magic had come in, he did wonder if his magic might be more than simply inconvenient. The exhilaration tingling through his body?

It made him feel powerful.

7

Nory and Elliott walked with Mitali, Anemone, and Fred back to the cabins. Once they were back in human form, Anemone and Fred turned out to be twins, with large brown eyes, teeth in braces, and similar upturned noses. Like Mitali, they wore sweatpants and T-shirts.

"We have to go change for dinner," said Mitali. She and Anemone turned toward the girls' cabins across the meadow.

"How come?" Nory asked, waving as Elliott and Fred headed to the boys' buildings.

"Uniforms," said Mitali. "Our headmaster's really strict. For athletics, we wear track clothes, but for all meals we have to wear jackets and white shirts."

"Everything neat and clean," said Anemone. "It's a private boarding school."

Nory shrugged. Her brother and sister went to a place like that—Sage Academy, where her father worked. They wore uniforms, too. "I can wait while you change."

The yard near the cabins was empty. Nory did a couple of cartwheels on the grass as she was waiting. She was relieved these new kids were so accepting, even though that was no guarantee that their classmates would be.

When Mitali and Anemone came out of the cabin, they wore crisp gray skirts, black Mary Janes, white blouses, and blue blazers embroidered with a logo.

Nory looked a little closer.

It was the logo of Sage Academy.

Father's school.

What? No!

Nory's stomach dropped. "Your headmaster—he's not here with you, is he?"

"Sure he is," said Mitali. "He always goes on the first-year student overnight."

Oh, yeah, Nory thought, remembering the tradition.

"In fact, we better run," said Anemone. "Snorace is really mean when people are late."

Snorace?

The two Sage Academy girls took off running in the direction of the cafeteria. "Come on, Nory!" shouted Mitali. "Let's zoom!"

Nory followed slowly.

Father was here. She wasn't sure she wanted to see him.

When Nory reached the cafeteria, Anemone had already gone in. Mitali was waiting at the door.

"Come with me," she said, grabbling Nory's hand. "I want to introduce you to our headmaster."

"Actually, I'm not sure that's a good idea," said Nory. The last time she'd seen Father, it had not gone well. At all.

"Huh? Sure it is," Mitali said.

They bypassed the line for food and crossed the cafeteria to the table where Stone Horace sat. He wore a corduroy blazer and tan trousers. A napkin covered his lap. Nory could see his close-cropped, graying hair and his strong, familiar jaw. He looked the same as ever. Next to him was a line of nervous-looking fifth graders in blue jackets. Nory knew they were waiting to shake his hand before they sat down with their trays of food.

Mitali walked fearlessly to the front of the line.

"Mitali!" boomed Dr. Horace, rising from his seat and clapping Mitali's shoulder. "How's my double-talent threat? Did kittenball practice go well?"

"Very well, sir," Mitali said. "I want you to meet my new friend Nory. She's even fiercer at kittenball than I am." She elbowed Nory in the ribs and grinned. "Well, *maybe*."

Father turned to Nory. His expression changed. Nory had been there all along, and yet it seemed as if he was only now noticing his own daughter standing next to him.

"Nory. Hello, my dear." He leaned down as if to hug her, then seemed to think better of it and reached out his big palm for her to shake. "It's, ah, good to see you. I had no idea Dunwiddle would be sharing our time at Dragon Haven."

"I didn't know, either," said Nory in a small voice.

"Mitali, Nory is my daughter," Father said.

Mitali's mouth fell open. "You're Elinor *Horace*? Dalia's sister?"

"Hard to believe, I know," Nory said under her breath.

"And in need of a cleanup, I would say," Dr. Horace pronounced. "You know to wash up before dinner, Nory. There's a spot on your shirt."

"Yessir," Nory said. "Excuse me, sir."

She turned around and hurried to the bathroom. There she scrubbed her hands with the rough paper towels until her skin stung. She tried to clean the spot out of her shirt and used the elastic on her wrist to pull her hair back into a ponytail.

When Nory returned to the dining hall, Mitali was next to Father with her tray of food. His face was alight with pride. Mitali was smiling.

Nory had planned to go back to Father's table. He *was* her father, after all, and she'd cleaned up just to please him.

But now she didn't want to.

She turned her back on them and went to sit with her UDM friends.

8

After dinner, Mo clapped sharply and announced the campers should bus their plates. They had thirty minutes of free time. Then everyone should meet at the fire pit for their first official dragon experience.

The students all headed for the doors.

Ms. Starr stopped Andres. She took his leash from Bax. "I have bricks for your pack," she announced. "Mo sent someone into town for them. Come with me and we'll get it sorted."

She reeled Andres down. Nurse Riley's backpack

was loaded with bricks now. Andres put it on, and sank to the floor—but it hurt. It didn't fit him well, the way his pack from home did.

"Good?" Ms. Starr asked.

"One less brick, maybe."

Ms. Starr took one out.

It still hurt, but Andres nodded.

"I bet that feels better," said Ms. Starr perkily. She patted him on the shoulder.

Andres smiled. He knew he was supposed to be grateful. But as he followed his teacher toward the fire pit in the meadow, he missed the freedom of weightlessness.

He and Ms. Starr were the first guests there. A young woman who was clearly a Flare was lighting the kindling, building a fire within a circle of stones.

Twenty minutes later, the flames were crackling and snapping, and the UDM kids were beside him. Andres glanced across the fire at Tip. Tip made a funny face. Andres grinned, and the evening got better.

Ms. Starr led everyone in campfire songs. She stood on a tree stump and got them all to sing "This Land Is Your Land," "Oh! Susanna," and other hokey classics Andres still kind of liked. A couple of Sage Academy Flare teachers lit sparklers. A couple of the fluxing students turned into kittens and chased each other around the grass.

After a while, Mo emerged from the forest that bordered the field. She carried a large box in front of her.

She put the box down several yards from the campfire. Flutterings came from within, and Andres heard a delicate, flutelike tinkling. Sebastian, who had worn his head cone during dinner, took it off.

"That noise," he said. "It's the loveliest sound I've ever seen."

"Luminous Dragonettes are famous for their firbling," Mo said.

"Firbling?" said Marigold.

"*Luminous Dragonettes?*" Sebastian said, his voice filled with wonder.

"Luminous because they emit light, like fireflies do," said Mo. "Dragonettes because they are one of the smallest dragon species we know about. These live in hives at one end of our property. They enjoy occasional outings, but they'll fly back into their box at the end of the evening. They know the box will take them safely back to their home."

Nory's dad, Dr. Horace, nodded. "Children, pay attention. There will be a quiz when we return to the academy."

"No one will have any trouble remembering these," Mo said. With a flourish, she opened the box.

Oohs and aahs rippled around the campfire. The Luminous Dragonettes were smaller than Mo's hand, elegant and long, with brilliant, iridescent wings. They swarmed into the night sky.

"That one—it glows purple when it flaps!" cried Marigold.

"And that one glows yellow!" cried Willa.

"Whoa," said Bax.

"They're miraculous flukes of nature," said Mo.

"The laws of science say they shouldn't exist, couldn't possibly exist, but here they are. That's why dragons are classified as magical animals, different from species we can explain with science."

Andres loved watching the dragonettes. He was entranced by their jeweled colors and their flashing wings. But he was equally content to watch Sebastian, who looked happier than he'd ever been.

"Miraculous flukes of nature," Andres heard Sebastian murmur. He caught Andres listening. He grinned. "Like us!" Then he closed his eyes and lifted his face, letting the dragonettes' bell-toned firbling transport him to another world.

Too soon, Mo was blowing on a funny-looking instrument to draw the tiny dragons back to their box. "Time for you campers to get to bed," she said briskly. She closed the box and locked the hinge. "We have a big day tomorrow."

The grown-ups threw buckets of water on the fire. Elliott, confident in his upside-down magic, iced several logs to put out their flames.

Tip and Phoebe clapped when they saw the freezing magic. Ms. Starr put her arm around Elliott. "You're letting yourself shine," she told him, "and it makes me happy."

"One more thing," called Mo. She was standing on the tree stump, waving at them now that the fire was out. "Tomorrow morning is pajama breakfast, a tradition here at Dragon Haven. Teachers and students, come straight to breakfast in your pj's, and bring your appetites. We'll have the grandest waffle bar you've ever seen. Strawberry syrup, whipped cream, fudge sauce, fruit. I promise you'll love it."

"Dude," said Tip, appearing by Andres's side. He held out his fist. "Waffles!"

Andres bumped his fist against Tip's. Dragon Haven was turning out awesome.

In the girls' cabin, everyone was in nightclothes. Willa had a fleecy pink sweatshirt and matching shorts. Marigold had a long blue nightgown that was surprisingly old-fashioned, given that she was usually a boots-and-leather-jacket kind of girl. Ms. Starr changed in the bathroom and came out in lime-green fleece pants and a T-shirt with a bunny on it.

Nory had brought her purple sweatpants and a short-sleeve sports jersey for the Pouncers, her favorite tigerball team. But she didn't feel like showing them off to the other girls. She felt strange to be sleeping away from Aunt Margo's. And Father was here, and she had barely talked to him. *And* she couldn't get comfortable in her bed.

Once everyone was under the covers, Ms. Starr turned out the light. Then she retired with a flashlight to her bunk on the other side of the room, reading a book and leaving the girls to themselves.

"The Luminous Dragonettes were so beautiful," Marigold said with a sigh. "Mo said we get to see them again, tomorrow night."

"I want to see them every night as long as I live," said Willa.

"You know what's cool?" Marigold continued. "The Luminous Dragonettes—when they firbled, it was like I could hear them inside my bones. I didn't even need my hearing aid."

"I think I heard it in my bones, too," Willa said. "I just didn't think of it that way until you mentioned it."

"Do you think, tomorrow, we'll get to see the big dragons?" Nory asked.

"My mom says this place has a group of Tangerine Dragons," said Willa. "They're supposed to be fifteen feet high!"

From far off in the forest, a tremendous and terrifying roar filled the cabin, rattling the wooden walls, and buckling the screened windows.

Nory's heart stopped. She forgot to breathe.

The roar went on and on, sucking away all thought or even the thought of thought. Finally, it ceased.

Willa spoke in a pretend baby voice: "I want my mommy."

Nory and the others laughed, but Nory knew it was not 100 percent a joke.

She stuck her head under the pillow. She didn't want to think about mothers. Her own had died when Nory was little. She had been a lovely mom, a doctor, a great tigerball player, a loud singer, a baker of muffins, and the kind of person who would always read just one more story before bed.

With her gone, Father wasn't much of a dad. He worked hard, kept the fridge filled with food, and kept the house clean. He *did* let Nory, Dalia, and Hawthorn have a lot of pets . . . but he was often cranky, and he didn't seem to know how to talk to his kids. He read bedtime stories, but only in a slow, boring voice, and only books he deemed educational. Father was opposed to graphic novels and sports on television. He was opposed to dirt and chaos and beaver lodges and squid ink. He was opposed to chocolate chip muffins, even.

Nory sniffed the air of the cabin for Father's scent. He usually smelled like coffee and sandalwood aftershave. Maybe he had come by, invisibly, to keep watch over her and say good night? He was a Flicker, after all. He could do it.

No. He wasn't here.

She was pretty sure.

She knew she embarrassed him. Her magic embarrassed him, her school embarrassed him, her hair embarrassed him, her shirt.

Father coming to tuck her in and make sure Nory was okay—that would be some magic, all right.

9

Zamboozle, the dining hall smelled good. Nory forgot to worry about Father as she hurried to the buffet line the next morning. Regular waffles, chocolate chip waffles, blueberry waffles. There were all sorts of toppings, too. Whipped cream. Maple syrup. Chocolate syrup. Strawberry syrup!

She felt a tug on her sleeve.

"Um, Nory?" Willa whispered. "Have you looked around?"

Nory looked around.

Ohhhh. Her stomach sank.

Mo and the kids from Dunwiddle were the only ones wearing pajamas. The Sage kids and their teachers were wearing their *uniforms*.

"Do they *sleep* in their jackets and ties?" Willa wondered.

"No." Nory knew they didn't.

Willa looked down at her own pink fleece. "They must think we're so stupid." She loaded her waffle with chocolate sauce, chocolate chips, and maraschino cherries. "What are they, too cool to wear pajamas to breakfast?" She shook her head and went to sit at the UDM table.

Nory felt like a deflated balloon.

"Good morning!" Anemone came up to the buffet. Nory nodded at her but continued making a sandwich of waffle, hot fudge, whipped cream, and then another waffle. Anemone's uniform was very neat. Her jacket was buttoned and her long brown hair was scraped back in a ponytail that made her big brown eyes seem even bigger. Would she make fun of Nory's sweats, slippers, and Pouncers jersey?

Anemone didn't say anything about it. "Did you see over there?" she said instead, clutching Nory's arm. "There's caramel sauce. *Hot* caramel sauce. I think I might move to Dragon Haven permanently."

Nory smiled. Maybe the Sage kids weren't *all* laughing at the UDM students. "Thanks for the tip," she told Anemone. She walked over and scooped caramel sauce onto her waffle sandwich. As she did, she overheard two Sage kids talking as they dusted their waffles with nuts and chocolate chips.

"Just like Headmaster Snorace to ruin the morning," one student said. "The kids from Dunwiddle must think we're the most boring kids in the universe."

The second Sage kid laughed bitterly. "Snorace the Bore—everything's always so dull when he's around. Mo said we could wear our pj's, and it's her camp. Who gave him the right to say we couldn't?"

Nory stopped dead in her tracks. *Snorace the Bore.* That's what they called Father. And he had forbidden the Sage kids to wear their pajamas to the waffle bar?

Wow.

Suddenly, the world flipped over. After years of living with Snorace the Bore, practicing for the day when she would wear the Sage Academy uniform, the strange fact of Nory's upside-down magic had landed her with a group of people who proudly ate their waffles in hot-pink fleece, granny nighties, and sports jerseys.

That made Nory feel . . . lucky.

Andres wore his new super-heavy brickpack to Rock Garden Creek, home of the Tangerine Dragons. An enormous fence separated the dragon enclosure from the common camp space.

Ahead of Andres, Ms. Starr, Nurse Riley, and the others gathered on top of a bridge that stretched across a canyon. In the canyon lived four Tangerine Dragons. They were recovering from injuries that kept them from living in the wild.

Andres stepped cautiously onto the bridge. He moved slowly with the weight of the brickpack.

"There you are," Ms. Starr said, taking his arm. She fetched a leash from her knapsack and latched it onto Andres's belt loop and the band he wore around his wrist. "Just in case. I still feel terrible about leaving your old pack behind. And then letting you *dangle* outside the bus! And then leaving you to be taken to dinner by the students from Sage Academy. I'm very, very sorry, and I have learned my lesson. I'm not letting you out of my sight, mister! Don't you worry."

Andres sighed. He felt like a dog, wearing his leash when his feet were on the ground.

Mo unloaded wooden crates of cantaloupes from the back of a red pickup truck that stood on the bridge. Nurse Riley helped. "It's a favorite food of the Tangerines," Mo explained. "And you students get to give them their breakfast."

Mo explained that Tangerine Dragons didn't fly. They mainly ate fruit. They were extremely large, though, and they tended to roughhouse. It wasn't safe for them to roam the property the way the Luminous Dragonettes could. Andres looked over into the canyon. There were three enormous, dusty-orange dragons wrestling and rolling around the banks of a creek that ran through the enclosed part of the forest. Each dragon was about the size of two elephants. They had huge mouths full of square-looking herbivore teeth, spiky tails, and tiny wings that didn't look good for much of anything. The largest of the three was a runner, snatching up cantaloupe after cantaloupe in his mighty jaws as Mo and the other students threw them.

Two other dragons shadowed the big guy and tried to get hold of his cantaloupes. They swiped at the melons with their claws, causing many of the fruits to roll away. Then the smaller dragons gave chase, batting and pouncing on them playfully.

Andres picked up a cantaloupe and threw it. The big dragon caught it perfectly and swallowed it after two quick chews.

"They're a clan, but I sense you've noticed that already," Mo said, appearing by his side.

"A clan?" Andres said.

"A family," Mo explained. "It's a mother and two children."

"That big one is a girl? Er . . . a *female*, I mean?"

"Sure. Having a family is rare for our dragon rescue camp. Go on, make it a game if you like," she called to the UDM kids. "Tangerines love to play with their food."

Nory gleefully pelted cantaloupe after cantaloupe over the bridge.

"This is *amazing*!" Elliott cried.

"That big one jumped fifteen feet," said Sebastian, smiling.

"The littlest one just stole a melon from the mom," said Willa, laughing. "Did you see? Right from the side of her mouth!"

"Don't you want to throw another cantaloupe?" Ms. Starr encouraged Andres. "This is a once-in-a-lifetime experience!"

"Don't *you* want to throw one?" he asked her.

"I'm happy just holding your leash," said Ms. Starr. "Really I am. You go ahead."

Andres tossed one in, but he wasn't feeling it. Ms. Starr was treating him like a baby. Yesterday, flying and swooping in the great hall while the Sage Flyers cheered him on, *that* had been awesome. Today, he felt weighted down by bricks and other people's worry.

His gaze landed on a lone dragon off by itself. He (or she?) was another Tangerine Dragon, the same size as the mama dragon who was catching the cantaloupes. The lone dragon's hide was more gray than orange. He had soft-looking scales, and skin that folded in a way that reminded Andres of elephants. His snout drooped. He seemed scornful of the cantaloupe madness happening all around him, and Andres noticed that the young dragons kept their distance.

"That's Ernesto," Mo said, her tone somber.

"He looks old," Andres said.

"Yes, but he's not as old as he appears. We thought housing him among the youngsters might energize him. Bring back his joy. But as you can see . . ." Mo let her sentence trickle off.

"Where's his clan?" asked Andres. The moment the question was out of his mouth, he knew the answer. "Never mind."

"These others never fully adopted him," Mo said softly. "He doesn't fit in."

A lump formed in Andres's throat.

"Why don't you go over and feed him?" Mo offered. "If you send cantaloupes his way, he'll eat them. The young ones don't have the nerve to try to steal them from him. Ernesto can be a grump if you try to take his melon."

Andres took two cantaloupes and walked down the bridge to stand close to Ernesto. He was so close he could hear the dragon's heavy breath and smell its fruity animal smell.

"Here you go, big guy," he said, tossing the cantaloupes down. Ernesto didn't stand up, but he scooched on his belly over to where the melons landed and ate them with a gloppy swallowing sound.

Ms. Starr was right behind Andres, holding the

leash. "That was nice of you," she said. "You're always looking out for the underdogs, aren't you, Andres?"

Andres wished she would just go away and not make *him* feel like an underdog. Or any sort of dog. But he didn't say anything.

"Ms. Starr! Ms. Starr!" Nory cried, running over. She was flushed. "It's Bax!"

"What happened?"

"He's gone missing!"

ndres reeled. Bax . . . missing?!

Nory's story spilled out, a confusing narrative about Elliott freezing a cantaloupe and Marigold telling him it was mean and Willa trying to take it from him because a frozen cantaloupe could seriously hurt a dragon. Sebastian said no, it wouldn't, and he'd really like to see the expression on the dragon's face when it realized the cantaloupe was iced. Nory usually sided with Elliott on things, but she didn't think you wanted to throw a frozen fruit at a dangerous animal.

She'd turned to look for Bax to see what he thought—and he *wasn't there.*

No one could remember when they saw him last. Nory said she was pretty sure he'd been there when they started throwing cantaloupes . . . but then again, maybe he hadn't.

"Ms. Starr, Ms. Starr, what if he got startled by the dragons and fluxed?" Nory cried. "If he's a swivel chair or a piano, we can find him easily. But what if he's *a rock?*"

Ms. Starr started to run, heading for the other end of the bridge where the rest of the UDM kids stood with Mo and Nurse Riley. Still on the leash, Andres had no choice but to follow.

"Bax!" the kids started calling. "Bax!"

They yelled his name, even though they knew that Rock-Bax couldn't answer them. But Boy-Bax could, and Piano-Bax could make sounds, so it was worth a try.

"He's always a big gray rock," Nory explained to Mo. "Like a boulder. So you can ignore, like, purple rocks and brown rocks and small rocks."

Mo nodded seriously.

Andres was terrified. It had not occurred to him that if Bax turned into a rock in the middle of the forest, he could be lost forever. Bax couldn't flux back into himself yet! And there was no way for anyone to know he was a fluxed boy-rock instead of a regular rock. Rock-Bax looked completely rocklike. He couldn't move or do anything.

Could Bax be that rock, the squat one nearest the bridge? Or maybe the gray boulder several yards over?

"Bax?" Andres called. "Is that you?" He couldn't believe he'd never noticed exactly what Bax looked like when he was a gray boulder. Did he have any dark markings? Any pointy parts? Any rough patches? Andres didn't know.

All the UDM kids were running from rock to rock, shaking them, thumping them.

Andres tapped Ms. Starr's shoulder. "Can I please unleash myself? I've got my brickpack on. I can do a better job of helping the others if I'm not latched on to you."

"Andres, not now," Ms. Starr said distractedly.

"Or if I took off my brickpack, I could search for Bax from the sky! I could get an aerial view!"

Ms. Starr turned in a half circle, dismay oozing from her pores. "There are so many rocks! He could be any one of them!"

"Which is why—"

"Keep up with me, please," Ms. Starr said. She strode off the bridge and picked her way carefully through the rock-littered meadow. "Bax is your friend, and you're worried about him. We all are. But the best thing *you* can do to help him, Andres, is to stay out of the way."

Nory felt terrible. How had it happened without anyone noticing? As Nurse Riley sprinted back to the main campground to get Bax's new medicine, she searched along with her classmates. She knew

Rock-Bax was charcoal gray and had a slight notch on one side of him. She and the UDM kids lined up all the rocks that looked most like Bax on the bridge, lugging them and rolling them.

Finally, Nurse Riley returned, panting from his run. He held a spray bottle full of inky liquid. He walked down the line of rocks the students had lugged to the bridge. "No, that doesn't look like him. No, not that one either. Oh, this one, maybe."

Nurse Riley sprayed the maybe rock.

It remained a rock.

Nurse Riley sprayed another maybe rock. No luck.

"I'm gonna ice them," said Elliott. "Maybe the ice will shock him into fluxing back."

"No," said Ms. Starr sharply. "You do *not* ice your friends. Flares do not flare their friends. Flickers do not make their friends invisible. Icing could really, seriously hurt him."

"I don't think so," said Elliott. "I think he'll be a

rock and then when he fluxes back, he'll just be kind of . . . cold."

"Elliott, do not ice Rock-Bax," said Nurse Riley firmly. "Just let me spray all of these, just in case. If he's not here, we'll keep looking for him farther along the path."

Willa and Marigold started singing. They sang everybody's favorite song, "Crazy-Daisy Shame." No doubt they remembered how Bax had once fluxed into Piano-Bax during that song. Maybe Rock-Bax would hear it and it would help him flux into Piano-Bax, which would make him easier to find.

Their singing made Sebastian cover his eyes and start rocking back and forth as if his vision hurt from the sounds.

Nory ran through the forest area near the Tangerine Dragon enclosure, searching for rocks that could be Bax. Her worry got worse and . . . *pop!*

She was a dritten.

That happened sometimes when she was stressed out.

There was no time for her to calm her mind and use what she'd learned in tutoring. Dritten-Nory had to keep looking for Bax. She flew over her friends, eyes peeled, looking for rocks she might have missed with her human eyes.

Suddenly, Willa and Marigold stopped singing.

How come? Dritten-Nory flew in for a landing next to Elliott. Marigold saw the dritten and shook her head in small, tight movements. Willa, paler than usual, pointed toward the path that led from camp up to the bridge.

Father and the Sage kids were standing at the foot of the bridge. "It's ten thirty," said Father to Mo. "Isn't this our meeting place for the Tangerine Dragons?"

"Oh, that's right," Mo said, rubbing her forehead with two fingers. "It's time to switch activities, but we can hardly switch now, can we? We're having an emergency with an Upside-Down Fluxer."

Nory's father stopped and blinked. "Was it Nory Horace?" he asked, looking concerned. His eyes searched the UDM kids and settled on Dritten-Nory.

Nory popped back into a girl out of sheer embarrassment. She felt washed in shame. *Drenched* in shame.

"No, Father," she said quietly. "I'm here. I'm fine."

His shoulders relaxed. "What's the situation?" he asked Mo.

Mo explained about Bax. Nory looked at Father. She saw him take in Sebastian's head cone and Andres on a leash. She saw him look at the way Marigold was shoving her hands in her pockets, something she sometimes did when she was worried she might shrink something by accident, and at a section of railing Elliott had iced while trying to demonstrate why it was a safe idea to ice the rocks.

She saw herself splattered in cantaloupe goo.

She saw Nurse Riley, his brown woolly sweater covered in inky Bax medicine, talking to a group of rocks and saying, "I promise I won't desert you. I just need to do you one at a time, so please be patient."

Nory could feel Father's judgment. She wished she were a Flicker so she could disappear.

"Are there still cantaloupes left? Excellent!" Bax's voice rang out loud as he jogged past the group of Sage Academy kids and over to the bridge where the UDM class stood.

Bax?

What?

It was Bax! Hooray!

Nurse Riley high-fived him, yelping with happiness. Ms. Starr started crying. Nory rushed to Bax and hugged him, all thoughts of Father forgotten for the moment.

"Where were you?" she gasped.

"I got chilly," Bax said. "I ran back to the cabin to put on a sweater and get my scarf." He looked around, taking in the long row of boulders, the Sage Academy kids, and the concerned faces of his friends. "Oh. Sorry. I guess I should have told a teacher, huh?"

"You think?" said Elliott. "We were really worried!"

Together, they breathed a sigh of relief, the UDM kids and their teachers. They piled onto Bax like

puppies, hugging and roughing up his hair and telling him the story of their search. Finally, he told
them to chill out and stop being so mushy because it
was going to make him yak and nobody wanted to
see that, he was pretty sure. Everything was back
to normal . . . if there was such a thing as normal in
the world.

11

Bax got a lecture on responsibility from Mo, Ms. Starr, and Nurse Riley. It was too boring for Andres to pay attention to. In the end, after all the boulders had been moved off the bridge again, the Sage Academy kids got, like, five minutes to look at the Tangerines. Dr. Horace didn't even let them throw cantaloupes, after seeing the UDM kids all covered with melon goop.

Afterward, in the Great Hall, Mo gave the students the option to choose their next activities.

"We'll be splitting into two groups," she explained. "But you get to pick what you want to do."

Andres saw Nory turn to Elliott. "Together!" she said.

"Together!" Elliott nodded.

"One group will go to the lake where our Bubble Dragons live," Mo said. "If you choose this activity, expect to get wet. You'll be boating across Greydrop Lake, observing dragons and learning about their habits and behaviors. Some of you might get to go water-skiing—two of our herd are being trained to work with the coast guard. They need all the practice they can get. Skimming across the water on the tail of a Bubble Dragon isn't for the faint of heart, but for those who are brave, there's nothing like it. And we have wet suits."

Excited murmurs rippled around the room.

"The second group will help injured whelps who are struggling with their motor skills," said Mo. "The flying breeds are having trouble flying. If you choose this activity, you'll be going to the Atrium of Healing, a vast enclosure made entirely of glass."

"Do you have to be a Flyer to go to the atrium?" asked a Sage student.

"You do not. There are activities for Flyers and Non-Flyers alike. If you want to go to Greydrop Lake, Luis will meet you at the east door, where Nurse Riley and Ms. Starr are standing." Mo pointed. "If you choose the atrium, join Dr. Horace and me at the west door."

All the UDM kids ran immediately to the east door to go to Greydrop Lake.

Phoebe, Lark, Tip, and Tomás went together to the west door. In fact, all of Sage Academy chose the west door. It was like Dr. Horace had told them to.

"Andres, come on!" Nory beckoned him.

Andres didn't want to go to the lake with UDM. He wanted to go to the Atrium of Healing. He wanted to see the injured flying dragons. He wanted to fly with them!

Tip jogged over. "You coming?"

"We can help the flying dragons!" Phoebe said, joining them. "And, not to sound harsh, but I don't think it's good idea to get in a boat wearing a backpack full of rocks. I mean, couldn't that be dangerous?"

"Andres?" Ms. Starr said. "I need you over here with me, now." She held out the leash.

"I'm going with the Sage kids!" Andres called back. He rushed out the door before she could stop him.

The Atrium of Healing was a large greenhouse with glass walls. It was filled with plants. The air inside was thick and tropical. Many flying dragons came from south of the equator. None of them breathed fire or hunted aggressively, so it was safe to be with them.

Mo gave the students a twenty-minute lesson on why certain orphaned whelps struggled with flying and ways the campers could help them. Many of the whelps had been injured. They hesitated to flap their hurt wings. They needed to build up strength—and confidence. Right now there were several different flying breeds living together, all young ones. The goal was to get them strong enough so they could be released back into the wild.

"Mostly they need encouragement," said Dragonologist Hendricks, who was in charge of the atrium. "Those of you who aren't Flyers, come over to this petting area. You can stroke them and feed them peanuts. Mimic the flapping movements Mo described. They'll copy you, and it'll help build their wing strength. Have fun—and I mean that. We don't have any adult flying dragons right now. These whelps have no one to show them how fun it can be."

Andres shrugged out of his brickpack, his spirits soaring. The moment his pack dropped off him, he was up in the air. He floated to the ceiling right away, but then he pushed off and worked on flying pur- posefully, the way he did with his tutor in the school gymnasium. The Atrium of Healing was much big- ger than the gym, though. *Way* bigger.

To fly down, Andres planted his feet on the ceiling and bent his knees. One powerful jump sent him shooting toward the ground. Hendricks had rigged the atrium with zip lines, so that the dragonologists could easily access tree-nesting dragons. Andres caught one and swung around it to change his direction. He did it again. And again! He could snag one with his foot if he got going too fast. He could propel himself from one zip line to another to another.

He hardly even looked at the dragons. He flew for the pure exhilaration of it. Tip and Tomás cheered him on. Then, remembering what he was there for, Andres pushed off the ceiling and found a low tree branch to hold on to. He grabbed on to the branch with his arms and legs and held on tightly. Nearby, Hendricks and Mo were talking to the non-flying students.

"The little green ones—see them?" Hendricks said. "They're called Arbor Dragons. Dragon Haven has six of them. They don't fly very high, but they seem to enjoy sitting on the zip lines."

"Like birds on telephone wires," one of the Sage kids said.

Hendricks nodded.

Just underneath him, Andres noticed a nest of leaves. Inside the leaves, a small Arbor Dragon was curled into a ball.

"That's Zog!" called Mo. "You can pet him. He's friendly."

Andres leaned toward the nest. "Hi, Zog."

Hendricks swooped to Andres's side. "Police officers found him on top of a lamppost in a crowded, bustling city. We don't know how he got there. The firefighters who rescued him told us he was trembling with fear, poor little guy. They sent him here for rehab."

"That's awful," Andres said.

"He *can* fly, physically. He's not injured." Hendricks sighed. "Instead, he stays in this nest, day after day. You can tell by his body language that he's still traumatized."

"But it can be fun to fly," Andres said. He

knew better than most how scary flying could be for someone who felt out of control. But he still pulsed with excitement from soaring to the top of the atrium. The ability to fly was a gift. Andres gazed into Zog's worried green eyes, trying to communicate all of this.

"Can I show you?" He held out his arm. "I promise to keep you safe."

"We've tried everything to tempt him," Hendricks said. "Treats, mainly. He's eating okay, but he will not—"

Zog stepped onto Andres's forearm, first one hind leg and then the other.

"Leave his nest," Hendricks said, his voice full of disbelief.

"Good boy," Andres said. "You're safe. I've got you. We're going to fly now, 'kay?"

Andres cradled the dragon gently against his chest and unhooked his legs from the branch. He bobbed to the ceiling of the atrium.

These whelps have no one to show them how

fun flying can be. That's what Hendricks had said. Andres's joy at his newfound flying skill was so strong, he could barely contain it. He didn't *want* to contain it.

But he didn't zoom around. He stayed with his back against the roof and tried to make Zog feel safe.

"You're doing it," Andres told the dragon. "You're up high and nothing bad is happening! See? Ooh, look at your pretty green wings. Those wings are made for flying—can't you feel it?"

Zog glanced down. His claws tightened against Andres's arm. Then all at once he spread his wings, pushed off, and swooped into the air.

Zog was flying! On his own!

Andres whooped. Hendricks let out an enthusiastic yell, thrusting his fist into the air.

Baby Zog flew around the Atrium of Healing, squawking with glee.

12

After lunch, there was an hour of free time. Nory was startled when Mitali found her by the water fountain in the dining hall. "Do you want to go explore?" Mitali asked. She hooked one ankle behind the other. "We could flux," she whispered.

Nory hesitated. She felt muddled about so many things. Almost losing Bax. Her dad being here. Mitali.

Nory did like Mitali. And she was interested in

Mitali's double talent. It was kind of like having upside-down magic.

Then again, Mitali was clearly Father's pet. The thought made Nory ache with jealousy.

Then again *again*, Nory wanted to see more of the fire-breathing kitten. And whatever else Mitali could do.

"Sure," she said.

Outside, the fall air had a buttery cast to it. Orange and yellow leaves fluttered. It was all so beautiful.

"Do you do any birds?" Nory asked Mitali. Almost nobody did birds till high school, but Nory had done bluebird and flamingo, both with other animals mixed in.

"I can do robin," said Mitali. Robin was a beginner bird, but a bird was a bird.

"Sweet! That means we can fly together!" Nory said. "I do bluebird, but I also add other animals to a lot of my fluxes. I can't help it, most of the time. So don't get scared if it goes upside down."

"Like how?"

"Last time I did bluebird, I added a touch of elephant and got really enormous." Nory grimaced. "Then I added a human face—we're talking a really big face, as in *my* face stretched out a hundred times. I'm pretty sure I scared the jellybeans out of everyone who saw me."

Nory thought back to the day she was Enormous-Bluebird-Nory-with-Nory's-Actual-Face. Blubiphant-Nory. She'd done all that for Andres, who'd been in danger. "I won't do that today, I promise."

Mitali laughed. "I can do elephant, but I've never done elephant and robin mixed together."

"Robiphant!" said Nory. "If you want to try, I think you'd just add a tiny bit of elephant to your robin. You take the elephant that's waiting inside you, and you kind of—let it out."

"I'm not sure my magic works that way," said Mitali. "It sounds cool, though."

"You know what?" said Nory.

"What?"

"Let's not talk about how our magic works, or Sage Academy, or my UDM program. Let's not talk about my father or double talents or upside-down magic. Let's not even talk about dragons. Let's just fly. Okay?"

Mitali grinned and fluxed into a robin.

Nory fluxed into a bluebird.

Together, they soared up, flying over the trees, over the buildings, and over Dragon Haven. They swooped and arced, looking down at the kids and dragons, ponds and meadows below.

Mitali was a very solid bird. She was good at holding her form. Ten minutes into their flight, Nory's bluebird turned flamingo pink. She caught a glimpse of her pink wings and felt her ego swell. Flamingos were *very* vain.

She was Fabluebird-Nory! Flabubird-Nory? In addition to being vain, flamingos didn't have the biggest brains—not that it mattered, given how fabulous they were.

Yes! Flabluebulous-Nory, *that's* who she was!

Flabluebulous-Nory and Robin-Mitali swooped and zoomed, leaving the weight of their problems behind. The air was surprisingly warm among the treetops. Much warmer than down below. The blue sky shimmered. Tiny pinecones dotted the highest branches like ornaments. Flabluebulous-Nory saw every detail up close: the sapphire sky, the emerald pine needles. She felt like she was soaring through jewels.

Finally, she and Robin-Mitali landed back in the clearing by the kittenball courts. Mitali fluxed back into her girl form. Flabluebulous-Nory circled Mitali once, making Mitali laugh. Then Nory fluxed back as well. Both girls flopped onto the grass, leaning back on their arms.

"So fun," Mitali said.

"Crazy fun," Nory said, breathing hard. Her chest felt looser, her muscles warm and stretched out. "I've never had a chance to fly like that before, out in the wild. I've only flown for a long time with my aunt, who's a taxi. Don't you feel lucky to be a Fluxer?"

"*So* lucky."

"Which do you like better, flaring or fluxing?" asked Nory.

"Neither, because I'm not choosing between them," Mitali said sharply.

Nory's cheeks grew hot. Had she said something wrong?

"Sorry," Mitali said. "It's just, your dad told me I have to choose one type of magic and stick to it if I can't keep them separate. You know, my kitten isn't supposed to breathe fire. My robin isn't supposed to make the temperature around me heat up."

"Is that why it was so warm when we were flying?"

"Yeah, I was flaring. But not on purpose!" Mitali shook her head. "I don't think your dad knows how hard it is to unmix them. It's not as if I haven't tried!"

"Father's pretty old school," Nory said. "I wasn't admitted to Sage Academy because my magic isn't one of the five Fs. At least, not the way the five Fs are supposed to be."

"I know," said Mitali. "I mean, your dad doesn't talk about it, but kids do. In the halls and stuff."

It stung to hear it, but Nory knew she shouldn't be surprised. Of course people talked about the headmaster's wonky daughter. How could they not?

"When my magic first came in, I tried *so* hard not to be . . . well, the way I am," Nory told Mitali. "But I *am* who I am, so now I focus on making the most of it. I mean, I can learn to control my magic better, and I can get better at the kind of magic I have, but it's never going to be typical." Nory thought for a moment. "I'm sorry my father can't accept you just as you are." She blinked hard. "I can tell he really likes you, though."

Mitali smiled awkwardly. "I know he's proud to have a double-talent student at Sage, but he wants me to be a *proper* double talent. He doesn't want me to flare while I'm fluxing, or flux while I'm flaring." She sat forward and drew her knees to her chest, locking her arms around her shins. "I feel trapped sometimes. Like . . . this'll sound weird . . . but like

I'm a slippery, oozy blob, and he and the other teachers are trying to squish me into a too-small container."

Nory laughed. It *did* sound weird. But she got it, because a while ago she and Elliott had read a book called *The Box of Normal*. It was all about taking "wrong" magic and pretending to hide it away inside a box. Nory had even tried the book's strategies, and it was just like Mitali said: trying to wrangle a large blob into a small jar.

The more time Nory spent at Dunwiddle— especially with Ms. Starr for her teacher—the more convinced she grew that "normal" was a dumb idea in the first place.

"You know what might make you feel better?" Nory said.

"What?" Mitali said.

"To do whatever you feel like doing without worrying about getting in trouble. I'm the only one who'll see, and you know I won't judge you for it. I'll even do it with you! Seriously, Mitali, let's just wonk out. Let's go for it!"

Mitali seemed unsure, but Nory knew she was right about this. She got on all fours, arched her spine, and *whoosh*! She was Kitten-Nory! She puffed out her kitten ribs, curled her kitten claws, and thought dragon-y thoughts. *Double whoosh!* She was Dritten-Nory!

She pranced happily. She flapped her dritten wings, making Mitali's hair whip about.

Mitali laughed. Still, uncertainty lingered in her eyes.

Dritten-Nory pounced and roared, a tiny flame shooting from her mouth.

Mitali bit her thumbnail, and then her body shimmered and shrank. She was Robin-Mitali again!

Dritten-Nory was delighted. A playmate! She made sure Robin-Mitali was watching, then flew toward the river. Dritten-Nory had an idea, but it involved being near water.

She picked up an autumn leaf with her teeth and tossed it in the air. Then she blew fire on it. Sparks glowed orange before what was left of the leaf hit the water. Dritten-Nory grabbed more leaves and tossed them at her friend.

Robin-Mitali hovered for a moment, and then *she* opened her beak and breathed out fire! The leaves burst into flame—glorious and shining. The sparks fell into the water, and the sizzling sound made Dritten-Nory's fur feel electric.

Robin-Mitali squawked. Dritten-Nory meowed. Robin-Mitali blew a fire bubble. Dritten-Nory popped it, and Robin-Mitali promptly blew more, a whole stream of beautiful, magical fire bubbles!

Robin-Mitali and Dritten-Nory circled and chased each other in the air.

They played until the bell rang for afternoon activities.

They had *fun*.

13

Back in the Great Hall, Mo told the campers they had three options for their afternoon activity. Andres was sitting between Tip and Phoebe, but he could feel Nory staring at him. Elliott, too.

Okay, he hadn't sat with them at lunch.

And he hadn't hung out with them at free time.

But seriously, did Andres have to hang out with the UDM kids every minute of every day? Was that part of the UDM rule book?

No. There was no UDM rule book.

". . . blahbitty blahbitty blah something about interactive online tutorials in the library," Mo was saying. "We designed this track for those of you who have expressed interest in the more academic aspects of dragonology. Not everyone wants to do fieldwork, and that's okay."

"Blech," Tip whispered, pulling a face. "*We* want to do fieldwork, right, Andres? We want to be out in the open!"

"Right," Andres said.

"Libraries are like cages," Phoebe said. "We're too wild to be caged."

"Heck yeah!" Andres said, his blood warm in his veins.

"*Shhh,*" one of the Sage girls said, giving them a withering look.

"We can't," Andres whispered. "We're too wild to be shushed."

Phoebe, Lark, Tip, and Tomás cracked up. Low fives were passed from hand to hand.

Mo moved on to the second option for the afternoon activity. It sounded far more fun than the library tutorials, even if it wasn't technically fieldwork. It involved visiting the dragon nursery, where clutches of dragon eggs were carefully monitored night and day.

"There are eggs in one clutch that could hatch at any moment," Mo said. "To witness the birth of a whelp is a once-in-a-lifetime experience—unless you're a dragonologist, that is."

Excited murmurs flew about the room. One look at Nory and the other UDM kids told Andres they'd be choosing that activity.

Mo laughed and held up a finger. "Hear me out before you choose. The third option is tracking and monitoring river dragons. This particular activity is geared to the Flyers among you."

"Say no more!" Tip cried, jumping to his feet. He looked at Andres, Tomás, Lark, and Phoebe, who scrambled up beside him. "Flyers reporting for duty!"

Some kids laughed. Others groaned. Mo tried to look stern, but even she couldn't resist Tip's eager charm.

Mo waved the five Flyers toward a man wearing green army pants. He had a handlebar mustache and forearms the size of hams.

"Andres!" Nory called. "Don't you want to see a dragon hatch?"

The man with the mustache pushed open the door of the Great Hall and strode into the sunshine. Andres followed.

The mustache man introduced himself as Blade. He drove the group of Flyers across Dragon Haven in a jeep. Veins popped out over his biceps whenever he turned the wheel. When they reached the river, he braked hard and hopped to the ground.

He passed out helmets. He showed them a speedometer and another measurement tool called a variometer. Then he asked, "Which one of you is the fastest?"

All four Sage Flyers pointed at Andres. Andres swelled with pride.

"Right, then." Blade tossed him the speedometer. "You take this. And remind me, you're the one who's upside down, correct?" He asked the question calmly, as if he was simply gathering basic information.

Andres nodded.

"In that case, hand me your leash and take off the backpack," said Blade, matter-of-fact. Andres gave him the leash, which Blade clipped to his belt. Andres floated into the air. It felt good to have the pack off.

Blade jerked his chin at Phoebe. "You're clocking the dragons."

He sized up Tip, Lark, and Tomás. "You three will fly behind us. What's your skill level? Two feet? Three feet in the air?"

"Three feet," said Tip.

"All of you? This isn't the time to stretch the truth. Some fifth graders don't get three feet up till the end of the school year. No shame in it. I just need to know so that I can keep an eye on you."

"We all go three feet," said Lark, lifting her chin. "We attend Sage Academy. The standards are *very* high."

Blade grunted. "Some of these dragons can jump two feet out of the water, see. And they're fast. When they find the current, they really get going. I don't expect you to keep up with them once they reach their maximum velocity. Shoot, I don't expect you to keep up with them at *half* their maximum velocity. But do your best."

"We will," Lark said, as if that was obvious. "But why does it matter how high the dragons can jump out of the water?"

Blade leveled her with his gaze. "Would you like to be hit dead-on by a dragon going fifty miles an hour?"

Lark opened her mouth, but no words came out.

"Exactly," Blade said. "These aren't cute little cantaloupe-eaters, people. Don't forget it for a minute."

Andres swallowed. The cute little cantaloupe-eaters were neither cute nor little, not if Blade was referring to the Tangerines they'd fed from the bridge. They were huge and hungry. He could only imagine how large and ravenous the river dragons must be.

Blade nodded curtly. "Those of you with devices, keep track of your measurements. If you don't have a device, your job is to observe, observe, observe. I want to know if any of the dragons look hurt, if any are having trouble swimming, that kind of thing. And remember, safety first. Levitation at all times. Three feet up. Got it?"

"Yessir!" the kids responded.

All six Flyers cruised along the river. Andres kept up easily with Blade, who was a very strong Flyer. Andres realized he had never before had his leash attached to another Flyer. Back at Dunwiddle, even his tutor stayed on the ground during their sessions.

Flying with such leeway felt wonderful.

"There!" Tomás said, spotting the first river dragon. Its large blue head peeked above the surface of the water. It blew a snort of mist out its nose.

"Let's clock it," Andres said, getting as close to the dragon as he dared. He pointed the speedometer.

"Two point five clicks," Phoebe called, checking the variometer.

The river dragon dove underwater and came up with a catfish the size of a cow caught in its powerful jaws. Andres and the others watched, mesmerized.

"There! Another one!" Tomás cried.

Together, Andres and Blade flew above the second dragon. She was a beauty, with sleek gray stripes highlighting the vivid yellow of her body. Faster and faster she went, and Blade and Andres matched her pace. Andres held the speedometer directly over her for five straight seconds.

"Forty miles per hour!" he called.

Man, it feels good to zoom like this! Andres thought. The wind whipped his skin and made him squint. Blade wasn't pulling him. He didn't need to. Blade was just keeping him from going *up* in addition to going forward.

"Andres! Blade! Slow down!" Tip yelled.

"Tomás is going low!" called Lark. "He can't stay three feet up and go so fast at the same time!"

"Shut up, Lark!" yelled Tomás. "I can so!"

"I'm tired, too," said Phoebe. "Can't stay up much longer."

Andres didn't want to stop. His mind, his body—*flying!*

But Tomás. And Phoebe.

And Lark and Tip.

Andres remembered being dragged along behind the bus when the UDM kids first started off to Dragon Haven. He didn't want anyone to feel left behind like he had.

He slowed down, and Blade slowed with him. They turned around and flew back with the weaker Flyers, staying a solid three feet above the water but greatly reducing their speed. Blade gripped Tomás's elbow and didn't let go, despite Tomás's protests.

As they flew, Blade pointed out some smaller river dragons who were floating on their backs like otters, glinting red in the afternoon sunlight. He also trained them to watch for the moment when a fast swimmer caught the current and surged forward like a rocket.

"Look how they ride on the current," Andres marveled. "It's amazing."

Blade nodded. "It's something we have in common with them," he said.

Later, as Andres shrugged into his brickpack so they could climb back into the vehicle, Blade clapped him on the shoulder. "You got some nice power there," Blade told Andres. "You take passengers?"

Andres shook his head. Then he remembered that he'd flown Tip up to the top of the Great Hall. "Well . . . once, but it happened accidentally," he said. "I think I could learn how, though. I'd like to."

"I took my first passenger at age eleven," said Blade. "But I dropped that kid in a sandbox, nearly broke half his bones. Turned out I could only hold him for a couple minutes. It took a good long while to master that skill."

"I can't even master going down," Andres admitted.

"So I've heard," said Blade. "Your teacher told me. But you'll learn how, just like I learned not to drop my passengers. Might not be easy, but you've got a lot of power, kid. You just gotta keep training. Check?"

"Yessir!" Andres said, and he saluted. He didn't mean to. It just happened.

Blade didn't laugh, or even smile. He lifted his hand from the wheel and returned the salute.

14

The non-flying Sage kids had all filed off to do the online tutorial. *The online tutorial,* when they were at an actual camp with actual dragons. So boring! Why would they choose that? Nory didn't understand until she happened to glance at Mitali.

Oh.

Mitali, Anemone, and the other Non-Flyers had looked to their headmaster to tell them what to do. And Father wanted them doing academics.

They could have learned so much more from Dr.

Nubbly, though! Nory knew that from the moment they arrived at the hatchery. Dr. Nubbly was a soft, round woman with flat hair, pale skin, and pink cheeks. She wore a Dragon Haven sweatshirt and didn't look glamorous, like Mo, or tough, like Blade. Instead, she looked whip-smart and cuddly.

"Remember, keep your voices low and calm," Dr. Nubbly told them as they walked into the hatchery.

In a small glass box sat a group of three glowing purple eggs, each the size of a grapefruit. Nory put her hand up to the glass. It was warm to the touch.

"These eggs," Dr. Nubbly continued, "are special eggs. All dragon eggs are special, of course, but Blurpers almost never hatch in captivity. These were found in a nest abandoned a thousand miles from here. They were transported in the back of a truck hauling soda pop and pretzels. Can you believe it? They're only a couple of hours from hatching. If they survive in this human-made environment, we'll get the chance to observe infant Blurpers."

"*If* they survive?" Nory said. "You mean they might die?"

"Are Blurpers the ones with huge talons?" asked Willa. "I read about those, I think."

"Sure are," said Dr. Nubbly. She turned to Nory. "We have high hopes that they'll hatch. They're fighters, and quite fierce. It's amazing the eggs are so small, isn't it? Now if, by chance, we're lucky enough to see one of the dragons emerge, I'm going to need you all to step immediately away from the box."

"How come?" Nory asked.

"Because whelps are like ducklings," Dr. Nubbly said. "They imprint on the first living creature they see."

"Imprint?" Nory repeated. "What does that mean?"

"It means to get attached," Sebastian explained. "A duckling is supposed to imprint on its mom, because its mom is the best duck to take care of it. But sometimes a duckling imprints on, like, a farmer or whatever. Then the duckling thinks the farmer is its mother."

"It is not ideal, not for the duckling or the farmer," Dr. Nubbly concluded. "Same goes for whelps. If an egg shows signs of hatching, we'll quickly box it up and take it to the Tangerine Dragon habitat you visited earlier. The mother dragon there will hopefully take care of these Blurpers, the way she cared for her own whelps. Blurpers can fly, but they're related to Tangerines and sometimes cohabitate. It's the best shot we've got, really."

"I've read about Blurpers, too," said Elliott. "They're kind of scary."

"They can be," Dr. Nubbly answered. "But a Blurper won't eat you, if that's what you're wondering. Blurpers don't have carnivore teeth. Their teeth are flat. Still, you don't want to be alone with an angry one—I'll say that."

The group watched the incubator for several moments.

The eggs sat there, being eggs.

"Moving on, then," Dr. Nubbly said. She headed

for a door on the other side of the room. "In the next wing, we have two Cuddlepuss whelps who are thriving. They have fur. Like rabbits!"

"Are *they* scary?" asked Elliott.

"You think that *everything's* scary," Sebastian pointed out.

"I do not."

"You're scared of dragons," said Sebastian. "Admit it."

Nory was at the end of the line. She dragged her feet, not ready to leave the Blurper eggs. Would the Blurpers really hatch soon? She wanted one more look.

She hesitated at the door. She could hear the others' voices growing dimmer. She'd take one last look, she decided, and then catch up.

She returned to the glass box.

Crack.

Nory's eyes widened. Had she really heard what she thought she heard, or had she made it up?

C-r-r-r-ACK! She heard it again, louder this time.

One egg, the smallest one, had gone from a dark purple to a lovely bright magenta.

"Dr. Nubbly?" Nory called. "Maybe you should come back!"

But Dr. Nubbly was in the Cuddlepuss room. Nory was alone.

The egg wiggled. Nory held her breath.

The egg jiggled.

There was one last crack, more of a *crickity-crack* this time, and a glowing pink line zigzagged across the egg. The two halves of the shell fell aside, and—

Wow. The dragon. The whelp, rather. It was pale pink. It nosed its way out of the egg and opened its large, dewy eyes. It was absolutely the cutest, most adorable, most lovable creature Nory had ever seen.

"Blurp!" cried the whelp. It was a teeny, tiny baby dragon roar.

"Hi, little bitsy!" Nory said in a talking-to-bunnies voice. "Hi, Roarie! I'm going to name you Roarie, okay?"

"Blurp!" Roarie trilled.

Blurp was right. Nory realized there was something familiar about Roarie. The shape of her wings and talons—that was it! Nory knew those wings and talons! She'd experienced those same wings and talons firsthand! Well, first paw. Yes! When Nory added dragon to her kitten to make a dritten, the bit of dragon she fluxed into was a Blurper Dragon! Definitely. A Blurper! Just like Roarie!

Nory put her hand to her heart. She knelt so that she was at the whelp's eye level. Roarie's eyes were round like lollipops. Roarie took a wobbly step toward Nory and trilled again. This time, her trill oozed with adoration.

Nory scrunched her toes inside her sneakers. Then, ever so gently, she removed the lid of the warm glass box that held the eggs. She reached the tip of her finger over Roarie's dewy head. Roarie trilled and nuzzled closer.

Ignoring her better judgment, Nory picked up the whelp and held it close. "You smell like pumpkin seeds, little Roarie," she said, leaning in and breathing deeply. "Pumpkin seeds and cinnamon! And grass!"

Nory knew she shouldn't. She really did know it. But Roarie was just hatched, and *alive*, and all alone. Nory couldn't just leave her there with no mother or father, teacher or aunt. Roarie was a Blurper! Nory turned into a Blurper! A Blurper kitten! A blitten!

Nory tucked the tiny dragon gently into the big front pocket of her hoodie and petted her through the fabric.

"I've got you, Roarie," she whispered. "Don't you worry. You're safe, and everything's going to be A-OK. I promise."

Roarie trilled.

Nory was in love.

15

Sitting with the Sage Flyers at dinner, Andres ate two helpings of spaghetti, five meatballs, and some broccoli, followed by a brownie and a peanut butter cookie. After his adventures with Blade and the river dragons, he felt very, very alive. Like a new boy.

Mo stood up with the microphone. "We have some urgent news. One of the Blurpers has hatched!"

Everyone cheered.

"Yes, yes, it's tremendously exciting," Mo said. "Unfortunately, the whelp somehow escaped from the nursery. He or she is far too young to be alone. If anyone sees the baby dragon, please let me or one of the staff know immediately. We need to ensure that he or she is properly taken care of. Thank you." She put down the microphone.

Andres saw Nory sink low in her seat, her hand protectively on the front pocket of her sweatshirt.

If he were sitting with Nory and the other UDM kids, maybe he'd ask her what was up. With Nory, something was almost always up. But he was with the Sage Flyers, and that was where he wanted to stay.

After dinner, Phoebe suggested the five Flyers go for a walk in the woods. She told the teachers where they were going and promised to keep to the paths. The sun was setting, but they all had their flash-lights. Andres wore his brickpack and had his leash in his pocket.

"Hey, Andres!" Elliott called as the Flyers walked past the UDM table. "Don't you want to hang with us in the cabin? We're going to tell ghost stories with Nurse Riley. Remember? On the back porch as the sun goes down!"

"Actually, I have Flyer stuff to do," said Andres. "I'll see you guys later."

"But we planned it," said Elliott. "Bax is going to tell us that story about the phantom hitchhiker."

"I have a good one, too," added Sebastian. "A real thing that happened to my uncle Panagiotis. It involves hamsters. Spooky ones."

"Maybe you can tell me another time?" said Andres. "We're going for a walk."

"Why is your friend wearing that cone on his head?" whispered Tip.

"Excuse me," Sebastian told Tip. "Not only can I hear your whisper, but I can see the sound waves *of* your whisper. They're a very pale green color, like the pee of an extremely sick person."

Tip had the conscience to look mortified. "I'm sorry," he said.

"People are always curious," said Sebastian. He sighed as if he were bored. "My head cone helps me cope in noisy environments."

"It's just so big," Tip said.

"Yes," Sebastian said testily.

Tip cocked his head. "What about blinders, like horses wear sometimes? Wouldn't that be easier? Or, I know! Aviator goggles. They wrap around your head and have dark sides so you only see what's in front of your eyes. Fighter pilots wore them in World War II! And they look way cooler than horse blinders."

"I am quite satisfied with my cone," Sebastian said. His lips moved in an odd way. "But thank you."

"Come on," said Andres to Tip. "The other Flyers are waiting."

Tip shrugged. "Okay. Let's blast." They bumped fists and left the cafeteria.

In the woods, Andres walked ahead, bouncing his flashlight against his palm. Everything that had happened at Dragon Haven was swirling around in his mind. He felt churned up inside. Then he made a decision. When they were solidly in the forest, with a thick canopy of trees overhead, he shrugged off his brickpack, holding it by his side.

"You're going to fly without it?" asked Tip.

"I can't fly *with* it," Andres pointed out.

Tip thumped his forehead. "Okay, then. Unsupervised outdoor flying." He grinned. "Dr. Snorace wouldn't approve . . . which means I approve completely!"

Andres grinned.

"I shouldn't be in charge of your leash, though," Tip said. "I'm too light. Phoebe, come over here and take Andres. He's going up."

Andres didn't want Phoebe to hold his leash. He didn't want Tip to watch out for him the way Nory and Ms. Starr did, either.

"Actually, I'm going leash-free," Andres told the Sage Flyers, trying to sound more confident than he felt.

Tip's eyes widened. "You can do that?"

"Sure," said Andres. "My teachers, they treat me like a baby. But with magic like mine, well—I can't spend my life tied down."

Tip looked dubious, but Tomás nodded. "Cool," he said. "Like tightrope walking without a net."

"No, like driving in a car without a seat belt," said Lark, shaking her head.

"The tree branches will keep me from going too high," explained Andres. "Chill out."

"I agree with Lark," said Phoebe. "I'm honestly not chill."

"Me neither," said Tip. "Not to be a downer, but no leash sounds dangerous."

Andres did *not* want the Sage Flyers acting protective of him. Protecting him or forgetting him—couldn't friends of his do anything *else*? Was Tomás the only one brave enough to back him up?

He dropped his flashlight, then his brickpack. He rose up, grabbing the branch of an oak tree and doing a loop-de-loop. Freedom! *Yes!*

Tomás levitated off the ground and tried to reach the same branch, but he didn't make it. He stayed solidly three feet high, and started zipping around at that height.

"Keep trying!" Andres encouraged him.

"About your leash," called Tip from the ground. "You're sure you don't need it?"

"I don't! There are so many leaves, they'll keep me from floating up!" Andres shouted. He pushed off one branch heading down, grabbed another, swung around, and flew into the air feet first.

He grabbed another branch, pushed off sideways and down, and swooped around his friends, who were all floating three feet up from the forest floor by now. "Sky tag!" he cried. "See if you can catch me!"

They couldn't. They couldn't go anywhere near as high as he was, though they zoomed and floated around beneath him, some of them vertical and some more horizontal.

Andres swung around another branch and launched himself higher.

"You're too good, Andres!" called Lark.

"We can't go up that far!" yelled Phoebe.

"Yeah, come down for a second!" Tip called.

Suddenly, Andres was above the trees. He had missed grabbing hold of the top branches.

Uh-oh.

"Andres?" Tip called. Worry tightened his voice. "Come down!"

Andres went up, up, up. Above him was nothing but cloudy sky, shot through with gold from the setting sun. Below was a carpet of autumn leaves.

Andres knew he was in trouble. If he couldn't find a way to go down, he'd just float away forever!

Think, he told himself. *Think!*

His tutor had taught him to kick like a swimmer if regular flying techniques didn't work. He tilted his body and swam as if diving down.

He still went up.

He imagined his body made of rocks, another technique from the tutor.

He still went up.

He imagined his body made of *lead*.

He still went up.

He imagined himself a helium balloon that was deflating, no longer able to float.

He still went up. What an idiot he was, thinking he could fly on his own!

Oh, how he wished now for overprotective Ms. Starr! She would know what to do. She'd call Blade or Mo, and one of them would come to the rescue. Andres even wished for bouncy, talkative, always-up-to-something Nory, who had once saved him by turning into a seriously wonky, elephant-sized bluebird.

He needed his UDM friends.

What a jerk he'd been, not standing up for Sebastian when Tip had whispered about his head cone. And for blowing off the ghost stories, which the UDM guys had been planning for days before the trip!

True, his UDM friends *had* let him bob helplessly behind a moving bus. And true, they had forgotten about him when he was on the ceiling and they were down below.

But just as true? They were his friends.

They cared about him. He cared about them.

He was crazy about them!

What if he never saw them again?

16

Twilight was coming on, but Nory was made of sunshine. Dragon Haven was made of sunshine. The world, the mountains, the forest, the universe—all of it was made of sunshine!

Why?

Because of one adorable-times-infinity whelp named Roarie. Roarie *was* sunshine, in dragon form.

Nory had brought Roarie to the empty kittenball court and watched the tiny whelp's first steps. Then her first flutters. Roarie had followed Nory all around the kittenball green. She tried to eat yarn and rolled on her back for a tummy scratch. When it was time for dinner, Nory had tucked Roarie back in the pocket of her hoodie. At the cafeteria, she'd fed the dragon tiny bits of broccoli, some meatball, and several spaghetti noodles. Roarie had eaten everything.

Now Nory took Roarie to the meadow in the evening light.

Who cared if Father was uptight and judgy and un-dad-like?

Who cared if he was Snorace the Bore and thought a person labeled "double talent" was more amazing than his own daughter?

Nory didn't care, at least not right now. She had a dragon whelp! In her hoodie! And it ate spaghetti!

She knew she would get in trouble if anyone saw her with Roarie. But she didn't care. She loved her little dragon.

The meadow was empty, as she had hoped it would be. The UDM boys were telling ghost stories with Nurse Riley. Marigold, Willa, and Ms. Starr were going over to the river to get a glimpse of the swimming dragons they hadn't seen yet. The Sage kids had cabins that weren't anywhere near the meadow, so Nory didn't think she'd run into them.

She set the whelp down on the grass. Roarie followed her wherever she walked, wobbling and fluttering. Nory stopped and squatted, wrapping her arms around her knees. She gazed into Roarie's lollipop eyes. Roarie gazed back adoringly.

"Blurp?" Roarie trilled in a tone as clear as a bell.

"Yes, you *are* the cutest dragon in the world," Nory cooed. "You want to be mine forever, don't you?"

"*Blur-bluepee, blur-bluepee!*" Roarie chirped.

Maybe Nory *could* take Roarie home with her. Aunt Margo wouldn't mind. Aunt Margo loved animals!

Nory would take such good care of Roarie. She would teach Roarie . . . well, she would read up on the things Roarie needed to learn. Roarie could sleep at the foot of Nory's bed. She could go to school with Nory and cheer during Nory's kittenball matches. And if anyone was mean to Nory? Once Roarie got full-sized, those people would run away and never come back. Blurpers grew larger than horses!

"And you know what?" Nory said, scooping Roarie into her arms. "If you were my dragon, I would never, *ever* send you away like Father sent me away." A lump formed in her throat.

Nory stood up and started walking, Roarie perched on her shoulder. Roarie's talons were sharp. They dug into Nory's skin even through the fabric of her sweatshirt. She'd probably have scratch marks, with real scabbed-over blood and everything. So what? She didn't care!

Wait.

What was that in the sky?

Her heart stopped.

It was Andres. He was high above the tree-tops . . . and rising.

Oh, no.

Was there anyone with him? That Blade guy or some other adult Flyer?

Nory couldn't see anyone.

Andres was flying solo.

Only, Andres *couldn't* fly solo. He would go higher and higher, until eventually he just . . .

Fear surged through Nory. "We have to save him," she told Roarie.

Roarie chirped and launched off Nory's shoulder. She hovered in front of Nory, her eyes filled with concern.

Nory fluxed into a dritten. Roarie trilled with surprise, but still seemed to recognize Dritten-Nory. *I can add some elephant later to help Andres*, thought Dritten-Nory. *I'll need to be bigger to save him.*

Zoom! Dritten-Nory and Roarie took off in Andres's direction. Nory flapped as fast as she could.

Andres floated farther and farther away! Dritten-Nory wasn't flying fast enough. She couldn't go any faster!

Poor Andres, she thought. *Hold on, poor Andres! I'm trying, I really am!*

And then . . . he vanished.

What? Where was he?

He had disappeared into a cloud.

17

The voices of the Sage Flyers were tiny, like mice.

The air around Andres grew cool and moist. He saw stripes of pink and fiery red. He'd levitated through a sunset-tinted cloud.

He laughed, feeling a bit like a madman. *Oh, sure. I've flown through a cloud—that's all.*

This was nuts! And it was very, very serious.

Think, think, Andres commanded himself again. This afternoon, at the river, he'd been able to fly with more control than usual. How had he managed that? Blade had held the leash, but that wasn't all of it. They'd been riding a current—a current of air above the river. That's how the river dragons swam so fast. They swam along with the current in the water and it made them zoom! The Flyers above them had been doing the same thing!

Current, thought Andres, whipping his head about as he floated upward. *I need to catch a current. Not a water current. An air current—and not just any air current. A downdraft.*

On the Dragon Haven campus, the wind nearly always blew from the east. Andres had noticed it because Mo always talked about the east door and the west door. Now, he knew the sun set in the west, right? So he could use the setting sun to figure out his directions and maybe catch an eastbound air current.

He turned. He reached his arms out. He fine-tuned all of his senses.

Nothing. He was still going higher.

Calm down, he told himself, trying to ignore his

racing heart. *Stretch out your fingers. Feel for an air current.*

Swooooooosh!

There! A downdraft—yes! The strongest, most wonderful downdraft he'd ever experienced.

Hello, downdraft!

Andres rolled onto it and rode it like he'd ride a wave in the ocean or a current in a river. Back through the pink-and-red cloud. Back past the tree line and into a drizzling rain! The downdraft must have come because of the approaching storm!

He grabbed the first branch he saw. The force of impact shredded his palms, and he didn't care a bit. He wrapped his arms and legs around the branch and held tight.

"Andres!" Tip called.

Tip, Phoebe, and Tomás were flying at full speed to the patch of forest underneath him.

"Zwingo, dude, you scared the stuffing out of us!" called Tomás.

Andres panted. His muscles trembled and quaked. He'd scared himself, too. Big time. "I'm okay," he said. "I kinda . . . well, I kinda lost control there."

"You think?" Phoebe said. She put her hands on her hips and glared. "You scared us to death! And we couldn't do anything! We couldn't do *anything* to save you! None of us even had a phone!"

Suddenly, Dritten-Nory arrived. She landed on Andres's branch, making it bounce. She was followed by a tiny pink dragon the size of a teacup. It landed on the branch, too.

"Nory?" Andres could hardly believe it.

She nodded, which didn't surprise Andres. Of course it was Nory. No one else was ever a dritten.

The others squinted into the tree. "What the heck?" said Tomás. "Who's the cat with wings?" He and the other Sage Flyers were still below.

Lark cocked her head. "And that . . . other thing. Is that a tiny dragon or a fluxed person?"

"Be polite," said Tip under his breath. "Andres's

friends have unusual magic! You can't just say stuff like that!"

"Nory?" said Andres.

Nory popped back into girl form. It was a neat trick, as she ended up sitting quite confidently on the large branch Andres was clinging to. She had a smear of spaghetti sauce on her sweatshirt. "This is Roarie," she said, stroking the tiny dragon's head. "She's a Blurper whelp."

"Ohhh," Andres said. "It was you! The whelp— Roarie. You took the whelp!"

"Yes!" Nory's smile brightened her whole face. "But more about that later. Are you okay? We saw you floating up and I came as fast as I could, but then you went into a cloud!"

"I was trying to fly solo," Andres confessed. "I thought the canopy of trees would protect me from going too high. I guess I was showing off. I hate having everyone watching out for me all the time. Like I'm a dumb baby."

"You risked your life," said Nory.

"I know."

"Please don't do that, Andres," she said. Her smile was gone. "Please."

"I'm sorry. It was a bad idea to fly solo, but when I was floating up, I figured out something! It has to do with air currents, I think. I was able to catch hold of a downdraft because the storm was coming."

Nory drew her eyebrows together.

"I'm really sorry." He fidgeted. "Go on and yell at me or whatever. I shouldn't have put you in the position of having to rescue me."

Nory stared at him. Then she grabbed her hair at the roots and shouted, "Andres, did you just say you caught an air current?"

Andres nodded.

"And you rode the current back down to the tree line?"

Andres nodded again.

A grin stretched back across her face. "Andres! You understand your power now! You can ride air currents to take you down when you're floating up!

That means you can do a million more things than you could do two days ago!"

"Yeah."

"I am so HAPPY!"

"Really?"

"This is such good news," said Nory. "You rescued yourself."

Andres took a huge breath, wondering at it all. "You're right. I rescued myself."

It was fully and truly dark now. The group walked in silence back to the main area of the camp. Andres wore his brickpack, and used his flashlight to illuminate the path. Nory stayed next to him, and the little pink dragon stayed next to Nory. The rain came down harder, and they all got pretty wet.

As they neared the Great Hall, Andres reached out and grabbed Nory's arm. "Hold up," he said.

Nory looked at him.

"I'm sorry I didn't sit with you guys in the cafeteria," he said.

"You didn't come to the Hatchery, either," Nory answered.

"Yeah, I know," said Andres. "And I skipped out on ghost stories. I think Elliott was bummed."

Nory shrugged. "It's okay to make new friends. I made a new friend, too."

"Yeah, but I kind of forgot the old ones."

"You did," Nory said. She studied him, then gestured to indicate the space between them. "But look."

"What?" he said.

She smiled. "You're here with one now."

18

"The rain's not going to stop, is it?" Mitali asked with a groan. "I wanted to see the dragonettes again."

It was what all the campers were thinking. They were supposed to go outside for the campfire and the return of the Luminous Dragonettes, but the rain had become heavy. Stormy, even. Everyone was damp and cold from the walk over, and now they were clustered in the Great Hall. Nory kept Roarie warm in her hoodie pocket. She'd considered hiding Roarie in the cabin, but she couldn't make herself do it. What if Roarie got lonely? Or lost? The hoodie was safest. Nory would be extra sneaky around grown-ups. That was all.

Nearby, Mitali directed her heating magic at the area where she, Nory, Willa, Anemone, and Marigold were sitting. Nory could actually feel her hair drying from Mitali's glow. Roarie even fell asleep.

Tip, Andres, and Sebastian were playing cards— and Sebastian wasn't wearing his head cone, even though the hall was noisy. Instead, he wore dark aviator goggles with blinders!

He looked proud and self-conscious, both. He also looked . . . well . . . not like a boy wearing a dog cone around his head.

"Blade let me have me a pair," Nory heard Sebastian explain. "He says the dragonologists wear them for flying at top speed. He said I could keep them."

"They're mad cool," Tip said.

Sebastian pushed the goggles higher on his nose with his forefinger. He swallowed and said, "The cone irritated the back of my neck. I appreciate your goggle suggestion. So, you know, thanks."

Nory spotted Elliott sitting with Fred. They were debating whether or not the Tangerines would like honeydew melon.

"It's green," Elliott argued. "I think they like *orange* things."

"It's still a melon," Fred countered. "I think they like melons."

"I wonder if they'd like orange cheese?" wondered Elliott. "Or orange sherbet?"

Nory glowed. Sure, everyone was disappointed about the rain, but it was cozy in the Great Hall. Dunwiddle kids were hanging out with Sage kids. The cafeteria staff had supplied after-dinner snacks. Carrot sticks, raisins, and spicy cheese zingers. Also Dragon Ball Soda, Plumberry and Cherry Bubblegum.

Nory heard Father's name mentioned, and her ears pricked up. She looked around, but she didn't spot him. He'd been here a couple of minutes ago, sitting on a bench over to one side, but now he was nowhere to be seen.

That didn't mean he wasn't in the room, of course. Father went invisible *a lot*.

". . . *such* a mcfoozle," Fuschia said, talking to a group of Sage kids.

Tip puffed out his chest, pulled his mouth into a sour-lemon frown, walked over to Fuschia, and said in his best headmaster voice, "Now, Tipperton McPipperton! You are here to learn about dragons, not to engage in idle chitchat. If you *work hard* and *do as you're told*—"

Fuscia laughed, and so did Fred and Anemone, walking over to the group. It made Nory suspect that her father had actually said those exact words in front of everybody.

"Indeed!" said Fuchsia, jumping into the game. She took on a headmaster voice, too. "Work hard and do as you're told, and you can accomplish anything, young man. But take a minute to make friends, spend one minute having fun, and you're sure to be a

TOTAL FAILURE. If you want to succeed, you must listen to . . . to . . ."

"The *dreadfully* boring words that spill so freely from my mcfoozly mouth!" Fred filled in.

Nory's stomach hurt. She wasn't sure what *mcfoozly* meant exactly, but she suspected it wasn't a compliment.

"He's so serious all the time," Anemone moaned. "Once, when I failed a math test, I got sent to his office. He lectured me about how I should appreciate the '*most noble of disciplines*'! As if my knowing geometry honestly mattered to him. He did this thing with his mouth like a toad."

Laughter rippled around the group of kids, louder and louder. Nory's pulse pounded in her brain. The Sage students flung insults at her father with abandon, giddy and rambunctious.

"A toad!"

"A bore."

"Such a mcfoozle!"

Nory bolted up, slamming her palms on the table. "Stop it! Just *stop* it!"

Everyone did.

Everyone stared at her, eyes and eyes and eyes.

"Dr. Horace is Nory's dad," Mitali said, so everyone could hear. She shot Nory an anxious, apologetic look.

"Oh, no," Tip said, cradling his head in his hands.

"He's still a mcfoozle," Fuchsia muttered.

"He is *not*," Nory cried, glaring at Fuchsia. "He's very smart. He's a powerful Flicker. And he works super, super hard." She swept her gaze around the room to include all the Sage students. "He cares about knowledge. He cares about Sage Academy. He cares about *you*." She pinned her stare on Anemone and said, "It really *does* matter to him that you know geometry."

Anemone blushed.

Nory knew how hard her father worked. She had seen him planning the curriculum at the desk in his home office, back when Nory still lived with him in Nutmeg. She knew he stayed up late having phone meetings. He worked on schedules and improvements for the school. She thought of the pictures she'd seen of Father with Mother, taken back before Mother had died. He had smiled big smiles, once upon a time.

When she spoke, her voice was thick. "He loves his job because his job is all he's got. His wife—my mom—she died. Now he's a single dad. He cleans and cooks and makes sure his kids do their homework. He goes to every event at the school. He meets with parents on weekends if they want to. He goes to sports competitions and magic exhibitions at Sage. So maybe there's not much time left for fun and games and silliness. And I know he's not always that nice, but he's doing the best he can, okay? You're lucky to have someone running your school who cares about education. Lots of kids don't have that. So quit being so mean."

Her muscles trembled. She spun on her heel and

rushed away from the table. She needed a moment to herself.

She stepped into an empty alcove lined with books. There, she closed her eyes and pressed her fisted hands against them.

She felt a change in the air pressure.

"Nory," her father said. He made himself visible and put his hand on her shoulder. "Will you look at me? Please?"

Slowly, Nory dropped her hands from her eyes. She turned around but kept her gaze on the floor. "Did you hear what I said to those kids just now?" she asked.

Father took Nory's chin and tilted her face upward. "I did. That was good of you."

"Thanks."

"My job is *not* all I've got since your mother died," he said gruffly. "I have my kids. They mean a lot to me. That includes you."

Nory felt shaky all over. "You hardly *ever* talk to me," she said. "I know I embarrass you."

"You didn't embarrass me just now, even though you *did* say I wasn't very nice. I was proud to hear you stand up for your family."

"I do stand up for you. I mean, I did and I will," said Nory. "But, Father, you don't stand up for *me*!"

"Nonsense," he said, sounding defensive. "I hope you know I pay for your after-school kittenball. I send Aunt Margo money every month. I sent her extra this month for a new winter jacket and some other warm gear. You know that, correct? And it's all because I want you to have an education that fits your upside-down magic."

"That's not the problem," said Nory. "The problem is, you don't call or text. You've only visited once and I could tell you were embarrassed at my concert because you didn't even come out for ice cream afterward. You sent me one present that Dalia actually picked out, and since we've been at Dragon Haven, you haven't come to tuck me in once, or meet my friends, or see my cabin!"

"Nory," Father said sternly. "I am *working*. Mr. Puthoor is here, and several other important members of our faculty. We are endeavoring to instill the values of Sage Academy in our new fifth graders. Any chaos or upside-down mayhem will disrupt my authority. Especially with Puthoor. He's not easy to work with."

"Father!"

"What?"

There was so much Nory might have said just then. She could have told him that no matter how busy he was, he could spare ten minutes out of his day to spend time with his kid. She could have told him that there might be opportunities for Sage students to learn *from* a little chaos and upside-down mayhem. She could have told him he shouldn't care what Mr. Puthoor thought, and that the students would respect him more if he showed himself to be a headmaster who was also a dad. She could have said, and maybe she should have said, "You should let everyone know that you don't love your stupid school more than you love me!"

She stopped herself before saying any of it. She took a deep breath and looked him in the eye. "I get it," she told him. "Work is important to you."

She *didn't* really get it. But she realized she might never *get* Father. And he might never get her.

He had his priorities wrong. He got embarrassed easily. He didn't like to mix work life and home life. He didn't like talking about feelings or difficult topics. He wasn't affectionate. Even though he was smart and hardworking, he was only a middling-good dad. Maybe he was even a lame dad.

Yeah, Nory would like Father to be fun. And generous. She wished he'd be nice to Ms. Starr, and that he wanted to meet her friends. She wished he could see there were advantages to upside-down magic, as well as difficulties—but he wasn't going to be that person. Maybe ever. Tiny changes and being nice to each other were probably all the two of them were going to manage.

"All right, then," said Father. "Thanks for under-standing about my job. I gather you'd like me to call you now and then, to see how you're doing?"

"Yes," said Nory, feeling this was a big step for him. "I think you should call me once a week on Saturday morning." She knew he liked schedules.

Father took out his phone. He programmed it in. "Phone call with Nory." He smiled wryly. "I suspect those kids are a little bit right. Maybe sometimes I am a mc—" He broke off, unable to say such a silly word. He rubbed his hand across his hair. "Do I care what my students think of me? Yes. A little. But a headmaster's job is not a popularity contest. And I am who I am."

Nory nodded. That was definitely true.

Then she had a brilliant idea. "You *are* who you are. Do you realize what that means?"

Father regarded her skeptically.

She plunged on. "Father! You're a really strong Flicker!"

"I am," he acknowledged.

"Which means you can save the night! Everyone's bummed about not seeing the Luminous Dragonettes again because of the rain."

"It is unfortunate," he said. "They're a natural wonder."

"But, Father, you could make the walls of the Great Hall invisible!" Nory said. "I doubt there's another Flicker here who's powerful enough. Would you? Please?"

"The students could observe the Luminous Dragonettes after all," Father said, understanding. "Seeing them in the rain would reinforce what we read about dragonette behavior patterns in different weather patterns."

"Sure. And they're beautiful."

"They are. They're beautiful indeed." He tapped his chin. "*Hmm*. Let me talk to Ms. Cho."

He strode off, stepping easily back into the role of brisk, efficient headmaster.

• • •

Five minutes later, Mo called for everyone's attention. When the room was silent, she said, "We have an unusual treat for you tonight."

Excited murmurs rippled up and down.

"Thanks to Dr. Horace," Mo continued, "we will be able to see the Luminous Dragonettes after all. They don't mind the rain, and now we won't mind it, either." She turned to Nory's father. "Are you ready?"

Nory's father raised his hands, palms turned up. "Students, direct your attention to the walls, please."

Puzzled, everyone did.

Father glanced at Mo, who turned off the lights.

The room went dark. Everyone gasped.

And then the room was filled with light. Not from inside the room, but from the world beyond the room. Nory's father had made the entire structure of the Great Hall invisible, furniture included, and now hundreds of glowing dragonettes could be seen swooping and looping outside. Trails of orange, blue, purple, and green made intricate patterns in the night sky.

Everyone was awestruck. Nory could see it on each face she looked at. Spontaneously, the room burst into applause.

The Luminous Dragonettes shimmered and shone. Raindrops reflected their glowing, multi-colored bodies.

Nory made her way to her father and stood beside him.

Father looked down at her and smiled. After a moment's hesitation, he put his hand on her shoulder.

19

At bedtime, Nory snuck a still-sleeping Roarie into the cabin and under the covers. Exhausted from her first day on the planet, Roarie slept through the night quietly.

Nory did, too. In the morning of her last day at Dragon Haven, she tucked the baby dragon gently into her duffel bag while she got dressed and brushed her teeth, making sure Roarie stayed hidden from Ms. Starr. Then she pulled on her same dirty hoodie from yesterday and tucked Roarie back into the pocket.

The sky was clear and blue. The storm had washed

everything clean. Dragon Haven was as beautiful as ever. Maybe more so.

I'll miss my bunk bed, Nory thought as she ate her scrambled eggs.

I'll miss this bacon, she thought as she ate her bacon. *And the waffle bar.*

I'll miss sleeping to the sound of dragons howling.

I'll miss brushing my teeth at a row of identical sinks.

I'll miss the meadow and the kittenball green and the paths and the lake with its Bubble Dragons.

She dragged her duffel bag over to the bus. Nurse Riley was already busy loading the luggage compartment.

I'll miss you, curb. I'll miss you, picnic table.

Nory hadn't seen Father yet this morning, but she spotted Mitali and called her over.

"It was so fun hanging out," she told Mitali as they clasped hands. "Give me your email."

Mitali did. "Maybe if you come home to visit, we can see each other? I live in the dorms when school is in session."

"Absolutely," Nory said. "I'll miss you, Mitali."
They hugged good-bye.

Nory left the parking lot and walked a little way into the forest, away from the prying eyes of Ms. Starr and Nurse Riley. On the woodland path, she let Roarie out for a walk. Roarie stretched like a puppy and then flapped and blurped about quite happily.

I'll miss you most of all, Roarie.

Tip appeared on the path from the boys' cabins. He approached Nory with his shoulders hunched and his hands jammed into his pockets.

"Excuse me," he said. "Can I talk to you?"

Nory bristled, but nodded.

"I'm sorry about last night," explained Tip. "What I said about Dr. Horace. Your, um, dad."

Nory waited, arms folded over her chest.

"I didn't realize he was your dad, but I still shouldn't have said what I said. Imitating him and everything."

"It was pretty rude," said Nory.

"I like to make people laugh, that's all. And I don't want people laughing *at* me, because I'm so short, so sometimes I . . . well, I shouldn't have. I'm sorry."

"Yeah, I guess so. Apology accepted."

Tip crouched down. "Is that your whelp? Can I pet it?"

"Sure," said Nory. "Go ahead."

Tip scratched Roarie's tiny head. Nory half expected him to scold her, to tell her she had to tell Mo about the whelp.

He didn't. He rose to his feet and said, "What Dr. Horace did, making the walls invisible and stuff— that was excellent. And he does care about the school. I can tell."

Someone cleared his throat. It was Andres, wearing his brickpack. "We're almost ready to leave," he told Nory. "You have to say good-bye to Roarie. Ms. Starr says so."

"Ms. Starr knows about Roarie?" Nory had kept the baby dragon hidden so well!

"Um, *everybody* knows about Roarie," said Tip. "All the fifth graders, anyway."

"Marigold really, really cannot keep a secret," Andres said.

Nory smiled. It was true.

"We didn't tell the dragonologists, though. Or the Sage teachers." Andres bent down and patted Roarie. "It's got to be hard to say good-bye. She's something."

Nory's eyes started to tear up. "It *is* hard. She just— she thinks I'm her mom! She doesn't *have* a mom!"

"She can still go live with the Tangerines," said Andres.

Nory started crying for real. She picked up Roarie and cuddled the Blurper. "I don't know if I can say good-bye!"

"I'll come with you," said Andres. "Come on. It's time."

Nory confessed to Mo about Roarie.

It was very, very awkward.

Mo wasn't mean about it, but she was not at all happy that Nory had kept a rare Blurper in her hoodie and allowed it to eat spaghetti.

But when Nory told Mo that she suspected her dritten was actually a Blurper-kitten, Mo got an excited glint in her eye. "Really?" Mo asked. "Can I see?"

Nory nodded. She scrunched up body and fluxed into a kitten. Then she felt her wings sprout. She shot into the air, Roarie close behind her.

After two minutes, Mo waved them back down.

Nory popped back into girl form.

"Wow," Mo said, nodding. "Yes, your dritten definitely has Blurper characteristics. I wish I had known that you flux into a dritten earlier in your trip so I could have observed you. Perhaps you could return to our reserve in the future?"

"I'd love to," said Nory.

Mo confirmed that Roarie could indeed live with the tangerines. She drove them to the bridge overlooking Rock Garden Creek, the place where they'd flung the cantaloupes their first morning.

They walked onto the bridge with Nory carrying Roarie. They looked over at the mother with her two younger Tangerines, super gigantic, rolling around like puppies, all three of them. They didn't need anyone. They didn't look like they wanted anyone, either. Especially not a tiny Blurper.

Andres shielded his eyes with his hand. "Look at Ernesto!" he said, pointing. "All by himself, just like the other day."

Nory saw the dragon Andres was talking about. She hadn't noticed him last time, even though he was bigger than two elephants, because of how he tucked himself into a shallow cave made of rocks.

"He has no family," said Andres. He sucked in a breath and turned to Mo. "Hey, could Ernesto take care of Roarie? Instead of the mama Tangerine?"

"That's not a bad idea," she told Andres. "In fact, it's a fine idea, and certainly worth a try."

"Roarie?" Nory said. She gazed into the whelp's lollipop eyes. "I have to go, and you have to stay here."

"Blurp?" Roarie trilled.

"You belong here with the other dragons. I belong back at Dunwiddle—that's my school—with other kids. And my aunt Margo. You couldn't live there. You're not a pet, even if you do love me a whole huge amount." She felt a bit weepy. "I have to say good-bye," Nory said firmly. "I'm doing what's best for you, so that you can be the best Roarie possible."

She hugged Roarie tight, then gave her to Mo. The dragonologist nodded and flew down into the rock garden with Roarie in her arms.

Nory and Andres held very still as they watched Mo set Roarie gently next to Ernesto.

Ernesto sniffed the tiny whelp, then lumbered to his feet and backed away. Roarie tilted her head and made a curious trilling sound. "Blurp?"

Ernesto watched her warily.

One of the young Tangerines ran by, followed by the other. The vibrations caused by their enormous bodies knocked Roarie off balance.

"Blurp!" she whimpered, sprawling. "Buh-luurp!"

Ernesto shook his enormous head at the young Tangerines. He made a low, gravelly sound and took two gentle steps toward Roarie. He bent down and sniffed her.

She sniffed him back.

Then Ernesto flopped onto his side, showing her his dragon tummy. Mo hovered over them. "That's a sign of trust and friendship," she called to Nory and Andres.

Roarie flapped into the air and flew a few feet to settle in next to Ernesto. She curled herself into a small ball and tucked herself in next to his neck, safe and protected from the rowdy Tangerine family.

"She's going to be just fine," Mo said as she flew back to Andres and Nory on the bridge. "They'll be good for each other, those two."

"I hope so," said Nory, gazing at Roarie down in the rock garden. "Could I please have a minute by myself?"

"Andres and I will head to the jeep," said Mo. "We need to get back soon, though."

Nory's teardrops splashed onto the wooden railing. They were the good type of tears. She knew she was doing the right thing. "You'll make a new life for yourself," she said to Roarie. "You'll learn dragon stuff, 'cause you're a dragon, and you'll get taken care of by somebody who's going to be really, really good at it, I can tell. And I'll come back and visit. This summer, maybe."

Ernesto's dragon tail was thumping the way a dog's tail thumped when the dog was happy.

Nory felt the air pressure change. She smelled coffee and sandalwood aftershave. Her father shimmered into view.

"Ms. Starr said you were up here," he said. "I wanted to say good-bye."

"Tell Hawthorn I miss him roasting marshmallows for me by hand," said Nory. "Tell Dalia I miss how she makes me laugh."

"I will. I know they'll be thrilled to hear of our unplanned reunion." He looked thoughtful. "Your teacher, Ms. Starr, gave me an earful just now about parenting. All I asked was where I might find you, *not* what child-rearing books I should read. She is full of opinions and ideas, isn't she?"

Nory nodded.

"I suppose the same could be said of me," Father said.

Nory nodded again.

Father ran his hand over his neatly trimmed hair. "I heard what you said just now, to the whelp."

Nory held still. Had he also seen her crying?

"Your observations were smart," he said. "And . . . you're making a new life for yourself as well. You're learning skills to deal with your upside-down magic, because like it or not, that's the magic you have."

"I'm happy with my upside-down magic," Nory told him. "I wouldn't trade it."

Father smiled and awkwardly patted her back.

On the bus, Nory took a seat next to Andres, who held his brickpack in his lap.

"Guess what I have?" he said.

"What?"

"Gummy unicorns. I found a whole bag of them at the bottom of my suitcase. My dad must have packed them."

"Zamboozle!"

Andres popped the bag open, and Nory took two. The cherry gummies were sticky, but she put them both in her mouth anyway.

After some fussing from Ms. Starr and Nurse Riley, and some grumbling from the bus driver because everyone was taking so long, the door finally hissed shut. The engine started and the blue bus chugged down the driveway. Sebastian opened his window and let the sun bounce off his spiffy new aviator goggles. Nory leaned across Andres and opened their window. She stuck her hand out and waved.

"Bye, Father!" she cried. "Bye, Anemone and Fred! Bye, Mitali! Bye, Dr. Nubbly! Bye, Mo! Bye, Roarie and Ernesto, even though I know you can't hear me! Good-bye, good-bye!"

When Nory could no longer see Dragon Haven at all, she shut the window. She stared straight ahead. Then she looked around, taking in the world around her.

The day was bright. Willa was laughing with Marigold. There were a lot of unicorn gummies to share.

Ms. Starr started singing "This Land Is Your Land," and Nurse Riley joined in.

Pretty soon everybody joined in. Even Bax.

The sun shone through the window, and Nory closed her eyes and let it warm her cheeks. She felt warm inside, too.

Also sadder, happier, wiser, friendlier, dirtier—

—and ready to be heading home.

Also by Sarah Mlynowski, Lauren Myracle,
& Emily Jenkins:

Nory, Willa, and friends return for another
upside-down adventure in:

UPSIDE⋆DOWN MAGIC #5: WEATHER OR NOT

Acknowledgments

Thank you with a double backflip and sparkly eyes to our editor, David Levithan. The people at Scholastic Press are numerous and magical: Lauren Donovan, Antonio Gonzalez, Maya Marlette, Lisa Bourne, Tracy Van Straaten, Rachel Feld, Sue Flynn, Lizette Serrano, Melissa Schirmer, Emily Heddleson, and Robin Hoffman—as well as a multitude of Flickers who make themselves invisible but whose work we appreciate nonetheless. Gratitude and gummy unicorns to our agents, Laura Dail, Elizabeth Kaplan, and Barry Goldblatt. Spicy cheese zingers for Bob, for all your salty support. Love and lemon drops to our husbands and kiddos (Anabelle, Chloe, Hazel, Alisha, Mirabelle, Maya, Ivy, Jamie and Al). And finally, a never-ending supply of Dragon Ball Soda for every single kid (and old-head) who reads our upside-down books. YOU make them possible!

About the Authors

SARAH MLYNOWSKI is the author of many books for tweens, teens, and adults, including the *New York Times* bestselling Whatever After series, the Magic in Manhattan series, and *Gimme a Call*. She is also the co-creator of the traveling middle-grade book festival OMGBookfest. Sarah would like to be a Flicker so she could make the mess in her room invisible. Visit her online at www.sarahm.com.

LAUREN MYRACLE is the *New York Times* best-selling author of many books for young readers, including The Winnie Years series, The Flower Power series, and The Life of Ty series. *The Forgetting Spell* is the most recent book in her Wishing Day trilogy. She would like to be a Fuzzy so she could talk to unicorns and feed them berries. You can find Lauren online at www.laurenmyracle.com.

EMILY JENKINS is the author of many chapter books including *Brave Red, Smart Frog*, the Toys trilogy (which begins with *Toys Go Out*), and the Invisible Inkling series. Her picture books include *Toys Meet Snow, Princessland*, and *A Greyhound, a Groundhog*. She would like to be a Flare and work as a pastry chef. Visit Emily at www.emilyjenkins.com.

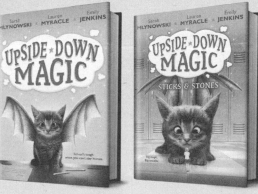